Be Very Afraid!

More Tales of Horror Selected by

EDO VAN BELKOM

Tundra Books

Published in Canada by Tundra Books,
481 University Avenue, Toronto, Ontario M5G 2E9

Published in the United States by Tundra Books of Northern New York,
P.O. Box 1030, Plattsburgh, New York 12901

Library of Congress Control Number: 2002101144

National Library of Canada Cataloguing in Publication Data

Main entry under title:

Be very afraid! : more tales of horror

Sequel to: Be afraid!
ISBN 0-88776-595-5

1. Children's stories, Canadian (English). 2. Horror tales, Canadian (English). 3. Children's stories, American. 4. Horror tales, American. I. Van Belkom, Edo. II. Title: Be afraid!

PS8323.H67B44 2002 jC813'.08738089282 C2002-900776-3
PR9197.35.H67B44 2002

We acknowledge the support of the Canada Council for the Arts and the Ontario Arts Council for our publishing program.

We acknowledge the financial support of the Government of Canada through the Book Publishing Industry Development Program for our publishing activities.

Design: Cindy Reichle

Printed and bound in Canada

1 2 3 4 5 6 07 06 05 04 03 02

To Anne and Frank,
my niece and nephew

CONTENTS

An Invitation to Be Very Afraid!

Edo van Belkom

People don't scare as easily as they used to.

Fifty years ago, teenagers went to the movies on a Friday or Saturday night, ready to be thrilled by stories of robot monsters, giant bugs, and big-headed aliens.

Today those things are campy. They make us laugh.

So what happened? What changed the way we get our frights?

Well, there are plenty of explanations for it, but one of the most important causes was the invention of television. Television brought the news of the world into our lives more quickly and graphically than newspapers, radio, and newsreels ever could. Suddenly, the news was more real than ever.

And the news wasn't always good.

As a result, people no longer had to go out looking for things to be afraid of. Frightening things could be found on a daily basis – around the globe, across town, and even on the block they lived on.

Today we don't have to head out to the movies to be afraid. All anyone has to do these days is . . . log onto the

Internet, ask a girl out on a date, try to fit in with the crowd, or act all grown-up.

This book is all about those personal fears – the fears we hold closest to our hearts, and the fears that cut us straight to the bone.

Each of these stories has its roots in the everyday lives of young people as they try to make their way in the world.

Diets.

Games.

Relationships.

They're all harmless-sounding words – almost boring, in fact – but in the hands of expert writers, they become subjects to be afraid of.

To *Be Very Afraid!* of . . .

Just One Taste

Randy D. Ashburn

The cardboard lady had been watching them ever since they walked into the mini-mart. Just standing there beside the cash register in a backless evening gown, staring over her shoulder and clasping between her fingers a long white cigarette that threatened to pierce her bright red smile any minute now. "Savor the Flavor of Elegance" was printed in gold across her. "Lucky Kings Ultraslim."

"You sure he'll sell them to us?" Andrea whispered to Chelsea, who was still pretending to page through *Teen People*.

The other girl waited to answer until an old man who was dragging something down the next aisle was far enough away. "Not a problem."

"I mean, you've, like, actually seen him do it, right? It's not just something Mandy *told* you about?"

Chelsea tossed her hair in that same old annoying way she had ever since she moved into the neighborhood in the fifth grade. "I bought a pack just last week." She switched the *Teen People* for a *Cosmo Girl*. "All we gotta do is wait till the store empties out a little bit, so the manager can't get into trouble."

The man behind the counter was stuffing a plastic bag full of candy bars and nodding at a woman with five kids, his smile as unmoving and unreal as the one on the cardboard lady in the evening gown. Above his head an icy blue banner declared, "Stay Cool – Smoke Arctic Menthols."

Chelsea crinkled her nose. "Gawd, if I ever turn into a sow with a litter of piglets, just promise you'll shoot me, okay?"

Andrea tried the obligatory polite laugh, but it came out sounding so much like a giggle that she wished she'd just kept quiet. It was too much to hope that Chelsea hadn't noticed, but at least she went back to the magazine without saying anything.

The old man in the next row wheezed and hacked like a dishrag was stuck in his throat.

Andrea spotted a picture of a boat in a storm on the window. A man was carrying a woman into the cabin, and despite the waves washing over the side, both had huge grins wrapped around their cigarettes. "Roanoke Lite 100s," the words under the boat read. "Just One Taste and You'll *Know* the Difference." She sure hoped whoever wrote that knew what he was talking about. So far, nothing else had made Todd realize she was more than just his best friend's "baby" sister.

Behind the ad, the parking lot of the mini-mart was growing dark. Of course night came a lot earlier now that they'd been back in school for a couple of months, but how long did Chelsea think they could hang out at the magazine rack before they heard that famous this-ain't-no-library speech?

"Chels, Mom's expecting me home by eight and –"

"Eight?" She said it like that was Andrea's age, not her curfew.

"Yeah, well, you know moms." Her head dipped toward her Nikes.

The woman with the bag of candy herded her children out the door. That left only the old man still in the store, and he was safely off in a corner mumbling to cans of dog food.

"Okay," Chelsea said, "if you're gonna go getting all nervous and everything." She put one hand on her hip and thrust the other one toward Andrea.

It took a while for her to realize she wanted money.

Chelsea took one look at Andrea's ten-dollar bill and plucked a fashion magazine from the rack. "Don't worry, you can see it when I'm done."

Andrea decided it wasn't worth drawing everyone's attention to tell Little Miss Obnoxious what a total snot she was being. Besides, if they took time out to argue, who knows how many people would pick that as the perfect moment to come in for a Slushie.

Andrea followed Chelsea to the cash register.

It was funny how every step they took seemed to get shorter and shorter, so that by the time they actually reached the manager, Chelsea was barely shuffling. She turned away as she slipped the magazine in front of him.

"Evening, ladies." He glanced down at the fashion model whose glossy eyes stared up from the magazine cover. "Anything else I can get for you?"

"Ummm . . ." Chelsea looked like somebody who was trying not to worry about who was watching. She grabbed a twin pack of Ho Hos so hard you could see the indentations of her fingers when she mashed it into the fashion model's face.

The manager's smile disappeared from one side of his mouth, like only half of him had the patience to wait for Chelsea to get around to asking for what she really wanted.

Andrea stared hard at Chelsea and nodded toward the rows upon rows of cigarettes behind the counter. She was trying one of those impossible things – moving her head just enough so that Chelsea would notice but the manager wouldn't. She stopped when she realized she probably looked like she was having some kind of epileptic fit.

"Oh, yeah," Chelsea finally said. "And my friend here would like a pack of Lucky Kings too. Ultraslim." She swallowed so hard you could actually hear it. "Please."

Andrea's mouth was moving, but no sounds were coming out. She stopped breathing. For hour-long seconds, the manager's eyes went from one girl to the next. Then he shook his head, reached behind him, and tossed a tiny box onto the counter. It landed with a muffled plop next to the Ho Hos.

When Andrea finally exhaled, it sounded so uncomfortably close to a giggle that she had to turn away. The cardboard lady in the evening gown still hadn't managed to get that cigarette all the way into her mouth.

Savor the flavor, baby.

"Coffin nails," the old man screamed. "Nothing but coffin nails you drive into these little girls!"

Andrea's heart jumped up into the place where her tonsils used to be. The old man was coming toward them, his hobbling steps probably the closest he could get to running. She couldn't believe they'd come so close to getting away with it, just to have everything ruined at the last minute.

The old man shook one frail fist in the air, and his nostrils flared so angrily you could see the scabs where yellowed tubes had been shoved up his nose. The tubes ran down the front of his shabby brown sweater to an oxygen tank that he dragged behind him on a tiny cart, its uneven wheels making it clank and yelp across the linoleum tiles like some vicious little dog nipping at his heels.

Chelsea was trying to disappear deep inside her middle-school jacket, and Andrea had already taken one step toward the door when the manager spread both his hands in front of him.

"Mr. Dmicek, please," he said. "I'm just trying to make a living here, you understand."

"A killing is more like it, yes? These girls" – Andrea jumped back so his gnarled twig of a finger wouldn't brush against her as he waved it around – "they are under the age. You cannot see this?"

The manager rolled his eyes. "So go find a cop. I'm sure they'll take time out from chasing real criminals to rush right over."

"Fah!" The old man leaned against the counter, trying to catch his breath. "Back home . . . there they know how to do the punish for the crimes, yes?" His voice could barely be heard over the beeping as the manager scanned prices.

"Well, Pops, maybe you just need to head right on back to the old country, then, 'cause over here we believe in freedom of choice. Somebody wants to smoke, ain't nobody else's business. That'll be $8.52, miss."

"Is *your* business, from what I am seeing."

Andrea couldn't decide how long they'd been standing there. Seemed like hours – probably less than a minute. Too long either way. Even if the manager wasn't afraid of the old man, what would happen if somebody else came in while they were still arguing? He'd never be able to sell them the cigarettes then.

Andrea made little shoveling motions with her hands, praying Chelsea would remember to give the manager the money before he changed his mind. When she finally got the message, Chelsea practically threw the ten-dollar bill onto the counter.

"Girls, you believe the lies he sells you with the cigarettes? Look at me." The old man gargled and growled around something all the excitement had pushed up into his throat. Andrea didn't even want to imagine what it might be. "Look at the face of someone who knows, my children. The chemicals. They put the chemicals in there so that one taste and they get you, yes? Just one little taste, and you keep right on making them rich even when you finally figure out they kill you." He pulled a half-empty pack of Laramie Filterless from his pocket and held it in his trembling, leathery hand. The tubes shoved up his nose hissed and sputtered as he tried to suck some air into the black and withered sacks that used to be his lungs. "This thing I know. Is not right to have to pay your own murderer."

Chelsea picked up the plastic bag with one hand and the change with the other.

"Please to listen, little girl," the old man said, reaching toward her.

Chelsea backed away, but her voice was barely shaking. "Sheesh, like, go back to the nursing home and take your pills, okay, Grandpa?"

He frowned so hard that his wrinkled face seemed to fold in on itself, leaving only those smoldering gray eyes staring out of the crevices. "One taste and you know truth. You see."

"Come on, Andrea."

"Show you like they do in old country, yes. You *all* see then!"

He was still yelling when they walked out the door, but it didn't seem much like English any more, and besides, all the coughing crowded out most of the words anyway. The whoosh of the automatic doors cut off the last of the sound, and Andrea exhaled long and hard.

They'd actually done it.

A moose driving a red sports car winked down at them from a billboard across the street. A cigarette dangled from his furry lips, the blue smoke around his antlers spelling the words "Destination: Satisfaction."

"Can you believe that freak?" Chelsea turned and marched toward Andrea, stiff-legged and with arms out like the Frankenstein monster. "Beevare zee coffing nails, leetle gurlz!" She nearly doubled over with laughter, but Andrea could still barely manage a smirk as she got onto her bicycle.

"So," she said, "where are we gonna, you know, do this?"

"Well, if you're in such a hurry, I guess we could just go around back. Assuming the winos haven't settled in for the night, I suppose we could hang by the dumpsters."

They sat down on the concrete steps at the back door of the store, and Chelsea emptied the plastic bag. The pack of cigarettes was gold and silver like a tiny treasure box, the cellophane wrapper making it sparkle under the dim light above the door.

Chelsea pulled out an old-fashioned silver lighter with a fancy *H* engraved on the side and laid it on the concrete while she tried to open the cigarettes.

"Where'd you get that?" Andrea asked.

"It's my grandmother's."

"How'd you sneak it out?"

She looked up from fumbling with the wrapper. "Chelsea Hill, master thief."

There was no way Andrea was going to risk three giggles in one night, so she just smiled.

"Like, she's a couple hundred years old, okay? Every time I go over to her house, she's asleep in fifteen minutes. Anyway" – Chelsea held up the open pack, its lid barely hanging on at one side, where she'd ripped it – "it's not like *she's* really supposed to be smoking either."

Andrea hesitated for just a second.

But that was more than enough time for Chelsea to screw her face into That Look. "Don't tell me you're letting that old lunatic get to you?"

"No! I mean . . . I dunno."

"He's just like my grandma and all the rest, you know? All they ever think about is dying, so they're not happy till that's all you can think about too!" Chelsea held out a cigarette. "I'd rather obsess about *living*, wouldn't you?"

The cigarette felt strange between Andrea's shaking fingers, and even stranger between her lips – stale paper on the tip of her tongue rubbing away the last hint of bubblegum. She jumped when the tiny yellow-and-blue flame from the lighter exploded right in her face, the fire dancing so near that she was sure she'd get burned. But Andrea leaned in close so the other girl would see she wasn't scared.

Chelsea was right: smoking was no different from bungee jumping or rock climbing. It was a way to stare right in death's tiny glowing eye and scream at the top of your lungs that you were alive.

But that first stinging mouthful wasn't really like smoke at all. More like fire crowding into her, crawling up the inside of her nose and singeing the bottom of her brain. Her eyes watered. She felt dizzy.

Worried what Chelsea might think, Andrea tried to suck the smoke in deeper, but it caught in her throat like an angry cat somebody was trying to shove into a burlap sack. Smoky claws dug in, scratching and slicing until Andrea was sure they were going to rip right out through her neck.

Chelsea laughed as she took the cigarette away. "Yeah, it's always like that the first time. You get used to it, though."

Andrea pressed her hands flat against the concrete and kept swallowing as hard as she could in between coughs, praying that the meatloaf and macaroni she'd had for dinner weren't about to make a second appearance on the steps behind the mini-mart.

Chelsea smiled around the cigarette. She looked so much older sucking on that glowing little tube, hardly coughing at all.

It didn't take long for the worst of the burning to go away, and Andrea found that the tingling that was left was almost . . . well, maybe "nice" wasn't quite the right word, but it wasn't all that bad either. Maybe she really could get used to it.

"Let me try again."

This time the bagged cat at least kept its claws in as it crawled down her throat. She tried taking long, deep breaths so there'd be no room left over for coughing. One puff. Two. Her head was a balloon slowly filling with smoke, floating up, up, up with each draw on the cigarette. Spinning. Drifting.

"Mmm, is the flavor country, yes?" The old man spat something thick and green between the two girls. It landed on the magazine, jiggling like Jell-O for a few seconds before it finally stood still right between the fashion model's eyes.

He was standing in the open doorway, the light from inside the building spilling around his dark form, blinding Andrea. Only the glowing little pinpoints of his eyes stood out from the silhouette, and thin lines of blue smoke drifted up from them in slow curlicues toward the October sky.

"Is time. A little taste of truth for little girls. You know then, I think."

Andrea was on her feet before Chelsea. That's probably why the old man's twisted and swollen fingers only skimmed across her shoulder instead of wrapping tightly in her hair as they did with Chelsea.

But one touch was all it took.

Andrea could feel the smoke of tens of thousands of cigarettes flood into her. Clogging her lungs with concrete. Filling her up with an entire lifetime's worth of *elegance* and *cool* and *satisfaction*.

And then the coughing came. It started somewhere deep inside her gut, not in those useless clumps of burned-up raisins in her chest. It was a jagged saw raking up and down her spine again and again and again. But no matter how hard she coughed – no matter how many fist-sized balls of thick, greasy slime she spewed onto the asphalt – the smoke was still there. Clinging to her insides. Hiding in forgotten places of herself.

But Chelsea wasn't so lucky.

She was shriveled, smaller. Her hair now more pale than blonde, so dry it snapped off in the old man's hands like uncooked spaghetti. Her face was the brown-gray leather of old, dusty shoes. Her coughing no more than a single unending, whispered wheeze.

Andrea jumped past the old man and through the open door, locking it behind her. But even that short run left her gasping like a grounded bass, desperately trying to shove even the tiniest hint of air down her tightly clenched throat.

"Help me." But she could barely hear herself as she staggered from the storeroom to the front of the mini-mart.

The manager was sprawled across the cardboard lady, his body covered from head to foot in nails – "Coffin nails," Andrea gasped – so that he looked like some roadkill porcupine.

Andrea collapsed into the racks behind her, an avalanche of cigarettes falling all around her. And at that moment she knew, really and truly *knew*, just like the old man had said she would. The worst part wasn't what he'd done to Chelsea or to the manager – or even to her. The worst part hadn't happened yet. It would come tomorrow, and for every tomorrow after that for however many years she had left. Because along with a taste of the smoke, the old man had also given her the hunger. The need.

Andrea sat in the pile of cigarettes, desperately trying to hold her hands steady enough to open another pack.

Driving a Bargain

Robert J. Sawyer

Jerry walked to the corner store, a baseball cap and sunglasses shielding him from the heat beating down from above. He picked up a copy of the Calgary *Sun*, walked to the counter, gave the old man a dollar, got his change, and hurried outside. He didn't want to wait until he got home, so he went to the nearest bus stop, parked himself on the bench there, and opened the paper.

Of course the first thing he checked out was the bikini-clad Sunshine Girl. What sixteen-year-old boy wouldn't turn to that first? Today's girl was old – twenty-three, it said – but she certainly was pretty, with lots of long blonde hair.

That ritual completed, Jerry turned to the real reason he'd bought the paper: the classified ads. He found the used-car listings and started poring over them, hoping, as he always did, for a bargain.

Jerry had worked hard all summer on a loading dock. It had been rough work, but for the first time in his life, he had real muscles. And even more important, he had some real money.

His parents had promised to pay the insurance on a car if

Jerry kept up straight A's all through grade ten, and he had. They weren't going to pay for the car itself, but Jerry had two grand in his bank account – he liked the sound of that: two grand. Now if he could just find something halfway decent for that price, he'd be driving to school when grade eleven started next week.

Jerry was a realist. He wanted a girlfriend – God, how he wanted one – but he knew his little wispy beard wasn't what was going to impress . . . well, he'd been thinking about Ashley Brown all summer. Ashley who, in his eyes at least, put that Sunshine Girl to shame.

But, no, it wasn't the beard he'd managed to grow since June that would impress her. Nor was it his newfound biceps. It would be having his own set of wheels. How sweet that would be!

Jerry continued scanning the ads, skipping over all the makes he knew he could never afford: the Volvos, the Lexuses, the Mercedes, the BMWs.

He read the lines describing a '94 Honda Civic, a '97 Dodge Neon, even a '91 Pontiac Grand Prix. But the prices were out of his reach.

Jerry really didn't care *what* make of car he got; he'd even take a Hyundai. After all, when hardly anyone else his age had a car, *any* car would be a fabulous ticket to freedom, to making out. To use one of his dad's favorite expressions – an expression that he'd never really understood until just now – "In the land of the blind, the one-eyed man is king."

Jerry was going to be royalty.

If, that is, he could find something he could afford. He kept looking, getting more and more depressed. Maybe he'd just –

Jerry felt his eyes go wide. A 1997 Toyota, only twenty thousand miles on it. The asking price: "$3,000, OBO."

Just three thousand! That was awfully cheap for such a car. . . . And OBO! Or best offer. It couldn't hurt to try two thousand dollars. The worst the seller could do was say no. Jerry felt in his pocket for the change he got from buying the paper. There was a phone booth just up the street. He hurried over to it and called.

"Hello?" said a sad-sounding man's voice at the other end.

Jerry tried to make his own voice sound as deep as he could. "Hello," he said. "I'm calling about the Toyota." He swallowed. "Has it sold yet?"

"No," said the man. "Would you like to come see it?"

Jerry got the man's address – only about two miles away. He glanced up the street, saw the bus coming, and ran back to the stop, grinning to himself. If all went well, this would be the last time he'd have to take the bus anywhere.

Jerry walked up to the house. It looked like the kind of place he lived in himself: basketball hoop above the garage, garage door dented from endless games of ball hockey.

Jerry rang the doorbell and was greeted by a man who looked about the same age as Jerry's father, a sad-looking man with a face like a basset hound's.

"Yes?" said the man.

"I called earlier," said Jerry. "I've come about the car."

The man's eyebrows went up. "How old are you, son?"

"Sixteen."

"Tell me about yourself," said the man.

Jerry couldn't see what difference that would make. But he *did* want to soften the old guy up so he'd take the lower price. And so: "My name's Jerry Sloane," he said. "I'm a student at Eastern High, just going into grade eleven. I've got my license, and I've been working all summer long on the loading dock down at Macabee's."

The basset hound's eyebrows went up. "Have you, now?"

"Yes," said Jerry.

"You a good student?"

Jerry was embarrassed to answer; it seemed *so* nerdy to say it, but . . . "Straight A's."

The basset hound nodded. "Good for you! Good for you!" He paused. "Are you a churchgoer, son?"

Jerry was surprised by the question, but he answered truthfully. "Most weeks, with my family. Calgary United."

The man nodded again. "All right, would you like to take the car for a test drive?"

"Sure!"

Jerry got into the driver's seat and the man got into the passenger seat. Not that it should have mattered to whether the deal got made, but Jerry did the absolute best job he could of backing out of the driveway and turning onto the street. When they arrived at the corner, he came to a proper full stop at the stop sign, making sure the front of his car lifted up a bit before he continued into the empty intersection. That's what they'd taught him in driver's ed.: you know you've come to a complete stop when the front of your car lifts up.

At the next intersection, Jerry signaled his turn even though there was no one around and took a left onto Askwith Street.

The basset hound nodded, impressed. "You're a very careful driver," he said.

"Thanks."

Jerry was coming to another corner, where Askwith crossed Thurlbeck, and he decided to turn right. He activated the turn signal and –

"No!" shouted the man.

Jerry was startled and looked around, terrified that he'd been about to hit a cat or something. "What?" said Jerry. "What?"

"Don't go down that way," said the man, his voice shaking.

It was the route Jerry would have to take to get to school, but he was in no rush to see that old prison any sooner than he had to. He canceled his turn signal and continued straight through the intersection.

Jerry went along for another mile, then decided he'd better not overdo it and headed back to the man's house.

"So," said the man, "what did you think?"

"It's a great car, but . . ."

"Oh, I know it could really use a front-end alignment," said the man, "but it's not that bad, is it?"

Jerry hadn't even noticed, but he was clever enough to seize on the issue. "Well, it *will* need work," he said, trying to sound like an old hand at such matters. "Tell you what – I'll give you two thousand dollars for it."

"*Two* thousand!" said the man. But then he fell silent, saying nothing else.

Jerry wanted to be cool, wanted to be a tough bargainer, but the man had such a sad face. "I'll tell you the truth," he said. "Two thousand is all I've got."

"You worked for it?" asked the man.

Jerry nodded. "Every penny."

The man was quiet for a bit, then he said, "You seem to be a fine young fellow." He extended his right hand across the gearshift to Jerry. "Deal."

Today was the day. Today, the first Tuesday in September, would make everything worthwhile. Jerry put on his best –

that is, his oldest – pair of jeans and a shirt with the sleeves ripped off. It was the perfect look.

He got in the car – *his* car – and started it, pulling out of the driveway. A left onto Schumann Street, a right onto Vigo. Jerry didn't have any real choice of how to get to school, but he was delighted that some of the other kids would see him en route. And if he happened to pass Ashley Brown . . . why, he'd pull over and offer her a lift. How sweet would that be?

Jerry came to the intersection with Thurlbeck, where there was a stop sign. But this time he was trying to impress a different audience. He slowed down and, without waiting for the front of the car to bounce up, turned right.

Thurlbeck was the long two-laned street that led straight to Eastern High. Jerry had to pick just the right speed. If he went too fast, none of the kids walking along would have a chance to see that it was him. But he couldn't cruise along slowly, or they'd think he wasn't comfortable driving. Not comfortable! Why, he'd been driving for *months* now. He picked a moderate speed and rolled down the driver's-side window, resting his sleeveless arm on the edge of the opening.

Up ahead, a bunch of kids were walking along the sidewalk.

No . . . no, that wasn't quite right. They weren't walking – they were *standing*, all looking and pointing at something. That was perfect: in a moment, they'd all be looking and pointing at *him*.

As he got closer, Jerry slowed the car to a crawl. As much as he wanted to show off, he was curious about what had caught everyone's attention. He remembered a day years ago when everybody had paused on the way to school as they came across a dead dog, one eye half popped out of its skull.

Jerry continued on slowly, hoping people would look over and take notice of him, but no one did. They were all intent on something – he still couldn't make out what – on the side of the road. He thought about honking his horn, but no, he couldn't do that. The whole secret of being cool was to get people to look at you without it seeming like that was what you were trying to do.

Finally, Jerry thought of the perfect solution. As he got closer to the knot of people, he pulled his car over to the side of the road, put on his blinkers, and got out.

"Hey," he said as he closed the distance between himself and the others. "Wassup?"

Darren Chen looked up. "Hey, Jerry," he said.

Jerry had expected Chen's eyes to go wide when he realized that his friend had come out of the car sitting by the curb, but that didn't happen. The other boy just pointed to the side of the road.

Jerry followed the outstretched arm and . . .

His heart jumped.

There was a plain white cross on the grassy strip that ran along the far side of the sidewalk. Hanging from it was a wreath. Jerry moved closer and read the words that had been written on the cross in thick black strokes, perhaps with an indelible marker: "Tammy Jameson was killed here by a hit-and-run driver. She will always be remembered." And there was a date from July.

Jerry knew the Jameson name – there'd always been one or another of them going through the local schools. A face came into his mind, but he wasn't even sure if it was Tammy's.

"Wow," said Jerry softly. "Wow."

Chen nodded. "I read about it in the paper. They still haven't caught the person who did it."

Jerry finally got what he wanted at the end of the school day. Tons of kids saw him sauntering over to his car, and a few of the boys came up to talk to him about it.

And just before he was about to get in and drive off, he saw Ashley. She was walking with a couple of other girls, books clasped to her chest. She looked up and saw the car sitting there. Then she saw Jerry leaning against it and her eyes – beautiful deep-blue eyes, he knew, although he couldn't really see them at that distance – met his, and she smiled a bit and nodded at him, impressed.

Jerry got in his car and drove home, feeling on top of the world.

The next morning, Jerry headed out to school. This time, he thought maybe he'd get the attention he deserved as he came up Thurlbeck Street. After all, even if the cross was still there – and it was; he could just make it out up ahead – the novelty would surely have worn off.

Jerry decided to try a slightly faster speed today, in hopes that more people would look up. But to his astonishment, he found that the more he pressed his right foot down on the accelerator, the more his car slowed down. He actually craned for a look – it was a beginner's mistake, and a pretty terrifying one too, he remembered, to confuse the accelerator and the brake – but no, his gray Nike was pressing down on the correct pedal.

And yet still his car was rapidly slowing down. As he came abreast of the crucifix with its wreath, he was moving at no better than walking speed, despite having the pedal all the way to the floor. But once he'd passed the cross, the car started speeding up again, until at last the vehicle was operating normally once more.

Jerry was reasonably philosophical. He knew there *had* to be something wrong with the car for him to have got it so cheap. He continued on to the school parking lot. Not even the principal had a reserved spot – it made his car too easy a target for vandals, Jerry guessed. It pleased him greatly to pull in next to old Mr. Walters, who was trying to shift his bulk out of his Ford.

Jerry was relieved that his car functioned flawlessly on the way home from school. He still hadn't managed to find the courage to offer Ashley Brown a lift home, but that would come soon, he knew.

The next day, however – crazy though it seemed – his car developed the exact same malfunction, slowing to a crawl at precisely the same point in the road.

Jerry had seen his share of horror movies. It didn't take a Dr. Frankenstein to figure out that it had something to do with the girl who had been killed there. It was as though she was reaching out from the beyond, slowing down cars at that spot to make sure no other accident ever happened there again. It was scary but exhilarating.

At lunch that day, Jerry headed out to the school's parking lot, all set to hang around his car, showing it off to anyone who cared to have a look. But then he caught sight of Ashley walking out of the school grounds. He could have jumped in his car and driven over to her, but she probably wouldn't get in, even if he offered. No, he needed to talk to her first.

Now or never, Jerry thought. He jogged over to Ashley,

catching up with her as she was walking along Thurlbeck Street.

"Hey, Ash," he said. "Where're you going?"

Ashley turned around and smiled that radiant smile of hers. "Just down to the store to get some gum."

"Mind if I tag along?"

"If you like," she said, her voice perfectly measured, perfectly noncommittal.

Jerry fell in beside her. He chatted with her – trying to hide his nervousness – about what they'd each done over the summer. She'd spent most of it at her uncle's farm and –

Jerry stopped dead in his tracks.

A car was coming up Thurlbeck Street, heading toward the school. It came abreast of the crucifix but didn't slow down; it just sailed on by.

"What's wrong?" asked Ashley.

"Nothing," said Jerry. A few moments later, another car came along, and it too passed the crucifix without incident.

Of course, Jerry had had no trouble driving home from school, but he'd assumed that that was because he was in the other lane, going in the opposite direction, and that Tammy, wherever she was, didn't care about people going that way.

But . . .

But now it looked like it wasn't *every* car that she was slowing down when it passed the spot where she'd – there was no gentle way to phrase it – where she'd been killed.

No, not every car.

Jerry's heart fluttered.

Just my car.

The next day, the same thing: Jerry's car slowed down almost to a stop directly opposite the spot where Tammy Jameson had been hit. He tried to ignore it, but then Dickens, one of the kids in his geography class, made a crack about it. "Hey, Sloane," he said. "What are you, chicken? I see you crawling along every morning when you pass the spot where Tammy was killed."

Where Tammy was killed. He said it offhandedly, as if death was a commonplace occurrence for him, as if he was talking about the place where something utterly normal had happened.

But Jerry couldn't take it any more. He'd been called on it, on what Dickens assumed was his behavior, and he had to either give a good reason for it or stop doing it. That's the way it worked.

But he had no good reason for it, except . . .

Except the one he'd been suppressing, the one that kept gnawing at the back of his mind, but that he'd shooed away whenever it had threatened to come to the fore.

Only his car was slowing down.

But it hadn't always been *his* car.

A bargain. Just two grand!

Jerry had assumed that there had to be something wrong with it for him to get it so cheap, but that wasn't it. Not exactly.

Rather, something wrong had been *done* with it.

His car was the one the police were looking for, the one that had been used to strike a young woman dead and then flee the scene.

Jerry drove to the house where the man with the basset-hound face lived. He left the car in the driveway, with the driver's door open and the engine still running. He got out, walked up to the door, rang the bell, and waited for the man to appear, which, after a long, long time, he finally did.

"Oh, it's you, son," he said. "What can I do for you?"

Jerry had thought it took all his courage just to speak to Ashley Brown. But he'd been wrong. This took more courage. Way more.

"I know what you did in that car you sold me," he said.

The man's face didn't show any shock, but Jerry realized that wasn't because he wasn't surprised. No, thought Jerry, it was something else – a *deadness*, an inability to feel shock any more.

"I don't know what you're talking about, son," said the man.

"That car – *my* car – you hit a girl with it. On Thurlbeck Street."

"I swear to you," said the man, still standing in his doorway, "I never did anything like that."

"She went to my school," said Jerry. "Her name was Tammy. Tammy Jameson."

The man closed his eyes, as if he was trying to shut out the world.

"And," said Jerry, his voice quavering, "you killed her."

"No," said the man. "No, I didn't." He paused. "Look, do you want to come in?"

Jerry shook his head. He could outrun the old guy – he was sure of that – and he could make it back to his car in a matter of seconds. But if he went inside . . . well, he'd seen *that* in horror movies too.

The man with the sad face put his hands in his pockets. "What are you going to do?" he said.

"Go to the cops," said Jerry. "Tell them."

The man didn't laugh, although Jerry had expected him to – a derisive, mocking laugh. Instead, he just shook his head.

"You've got no evidence."

"The car slows down on its own every time I pass the spot where the" – he'd been about to say "accident," but that was the wrong word – "where the *crime* occurred."

This time, the man's face did show a reaction, a lifting of his shaggy, graying eyebrows. "Really?" But he composed himself quickly. "The police won't give you the time of day if you come in with a crazy story like that."

"Maybe," said Jerry, trying to sound more confident than he felt. "Maybe not."

"Look, I've been nice to you," said the man. "I gave you a great deal on that car."

"Of course you did!" snapped Jerry. "You wanted to get rid of it! After what you did –"

"I told you, son, I didn't do anything."

"That girl – Tammy – she can't rest, you know. She's reaching out from beyond the grave, trying to stop that car every time it passes that spot. You've got to turn yourself in. You've got to let her rest."

"Get out of here, kid. Leave me alone."

"I can't," said Jerry. "I can't because it won't leave *her* alone. You have to go to the police and tell them what you did."

"How many times do I have to tell you? I didn't do anything!" The old man turned around for a second, and Jerry thought he was going to disappear into the house. But he didn't; he simply grabbed a hockey stick that must have been leaning against a wall just inside the door. He raised the stick menacingly. "Now get out of here!" he shouted.

Jerry couldn't believe the man was going to chase him down the street, in full view of his neighbors. "You have to turn yourself in," he said firmly.

The man took a swing at him – high-sticking, indeed! – and Jerry started running for his car. The old guy continued after him. Jerry scrambled into the driver's seat and slammed the door behind him. He threw the car into reverse, but not before the man brought the hockey stick down on the front of the hood – somewhere near, Jerry felt sure, the spot where the car had crashed into poor Tammy Jameson.

Jerry had no idea what was the right thing to do. He suspected that the basset hound was correct: the police would laugh him out of the station if he came to them with his story. Of course, if they'd just *try* driving his car along Thurlbeck, they'd see for themselves. But adults were so smug; no matter how much he begged, they'd refuse.

And so Jerry found himself doing something that might have been stupid. He should have been at home studying – or even better, out on a date with Ashley Brown. Instead, he was parked on the side of the street, a few doors up from the man's house, from the driveway that used to be home to this car. He didn't know exactly what he was doing. Did they call this casing the joint? No, that was when you were planning a robbery. Ah, he had it! A stakeout. Cool.

Jerry waited. It was dark enough to see a few stars – and he hoped that meant it was also dark enough that the old man wouldn't see him, even if he glanced out his front window.

Jerry wasn't even sure what he was waiting for. It was just like Ms. Singh, his chemistry teacher, said: he'd know it when he saw it.

And at last *it* appeared.

Jerry felt like slapping his hand against his forehead, but a theatrical gesture like that was wasted when there was no one around to see it. Still, he wondered how he could have been so stupid.

That old man wasn't the one who'd used the hockey stick. Oh, he might have dented Jerry's hood with it, but the dents in the garage door were the work of someone else.

And that someone else was walking up the driveway, hands shoved deep into the pockets of a blue leather jacket, dark-haired head downcast. He looked maybe a year or two older than Jerry.

Of course, it could have been a delivery person or something. But no, Jerry could see the guy take out a set of keys and let himself into the house. And for one brief moment, he saw the guy's face, a long face, a sad face . . . but a young face.

The car hadn't belonged to the old man. It had belonged to his son.

There were fifteen hundred kids at Eastern High. No reason Jerry should know them all on sight – especially ones who weren't in his grade. Oh, he knew the names of all the babes in grade twelve – he and the other boys his age fantasized about them often enough – but some long-faced guy with dark hair? Jerry wouldn't have paid any attention to him.

Until now.

It was three days before he caught sight of the guy walking the halls at Eastern. His last name, Jerry knew, was likely Forsythe, since that was the old man's name, the name Jerry had written on the check for the car. It wasn't much longer before he had found where young Forsythe's locker was located. And then Jerry cut his last class – history, which he could easily afford to miss once – and waited in a stairwell, where he could keep an eye on Forsythe's locker.

At about 3:35, Forsythe came up to it, dialed the combo,

put some books inside, took out a couple of others, and put on the same blue leather jacket Jerry had seen him in the night of his stakeout. And then he started walking out.

Jerry watched him head out, then he hurried to the parking lot and got into the Toyota.

Jerry was crawling along – and this time, it was of his own volition. He didn't want to overtake Forsythe – not yet. But then Forsythe did something completely unexpected. Instead of walking down Thurlbeck, he headed in the opposite direction, away from his own house. Could it be that Jerry was wrong about who this was? After all, he'd seen Forsythe's son only once before, on a dark night, and –

No. It came to him in a flash what Forsythe was doing. He was going to walk the long way around – a full mile out of his way – so that he wouldn't have to go past the spot where he'd hit Tammy Jameson.

Jerry wondered if he'd avoided the spot entirely since hitting her or had got cold feet only once the cross had been erected. He rolled down his window, followed Forsythe, and pulled up next to him, matching his car's velocity to Forsythe's walking speed.

"Hey," said Jerry.

The other guy looked up and his eyes went wide in recognition – not of Jerry, but of what had once been his car.

"What?" said Forsythe.

"You look like you could use a lift," said Jerry.

"Naw. I live just up there." He waved vaguely ahead of him.

"No, you don't," said Jerry, and he recited the address he'd gone to to buy the car.

"What do you want?" said Forsythe.

"Your old man gave me a good deal on this car," said Jerry. "And I figured out why."

Forsythe shook his head. "I don't know what you're talking about."

"Yes, you do. I know you do." He paused. "*She* knows you do."

The guy told Jerry to go . . . well, to go do something that was physically impossible. Jerry's heart was racing, but he tried to sound cool. "Sooner or later, you'll want to come clean on this."

Forsythe said nothing.

"Maybe tomorrow," said Jerry, and he drove off.

❦

That night, Jerry went to the hardware store to get the stuff he needed. Of course, he couldn't do anything about it early in the day; someone might come along. So he waited until his final period – which today was English – and he cut class again. He then went out to his car, got what he needed from the trunk, and went up Thurlbeck.

When he was done, he returned to the parking lot and waited for Forsythe to head out for home.

❦

Jerry finally caught sight of Forsythe. Just as he had the day before, Forsythe walked to the edge of the schoolyard. But there he hesitated for a moment, as if wondering if he dared take the short way home. But he apparently couldn't do that. He took a deep breath and headed up Thurlbeck.

Jerry started his car but lagged behind Forsythe, crawling along, his foot barely touching the accelerator.

There was a large pine tree up ahead. Jerry waited for Forsythe to come abreast of it and . . .

The disadvantage of following Forsythe was that Jerry couldn't see the other kid's face when he caught sight of the new cross Jerry had banged together and sunk into the grass next to the sidewalk. But he saw Forsythe stop dead in his tracks.

Just as *she* had been stopped dead in his tracks.

Jerry saw Forsythe loom in, look at the words written not in black, as on Tammy's cross, but in red – words that said, "Our sins testify against us."

Forsythe began to run ahead, panicking, and Jerry pressed down a little more on the accelerator, keeping up. All those years of Sunday school were coming in handy.

Forsythe came to another tree. In its lee, he surely could see the second wooden cross, with its letters as crimson as blood: "He shall make amends for the harm he hath done."

Forsythe was swinging his head left and right, clearly terrified. But he continued running forward.

A third tree. A third cross. And a third red message, the simplest of all: "Thou shalt not kill."

Finally, Forsythe turned around and caught sight of Jerry.

Jerry sped up, coming alongside him. Forsythe's face was a mask of terror. Jerry rolled down his window, leaned an elbow out, and said, as nonchalantly as he could manage, "Going my way?"

Forsythe clearly didn't know what to say. He looked up ahead, apparently wondering if there were more crosses to come. Then he turned and looked back the other way, off into the distance.

"There's just one down the other way," said Jerry. "If you'd prefer to walk by it . . ."

Forsythe swore at Jerry, but without much force. "What's this to you?" he snapped.

"I want her to let my car go. I worked my tail off for these wheels."

Forsythe stared at him, the way you'd look at somebody who might be crazy.

"So," said Jerry, again trying for an offhand tone, "going my way?"

Forsythe was quiet for a long moment. "Depends where you're going," he said at last.

"Oh, I thought I'd take a swing by the police station," Jerry said.

Forsythe looked up Thurlbeck once more, then down it, then at last back at Jerry. He shrugged, but it wasn't as if he was unsure. Rather, it was as if he was shucking a giant weight from his shoulders.

"Yeah," he said to Jerry. "Yeah, I could use a lift."

Darkness

Edmund Plante

Darkness.

That's all Gabrielle McIntyre could see ahead of her. Nothingness. Darkness. Blackness.

"Hey, Gabby, if you're not going to eat that, can I?"

It took Gabrielle more than a second to surface and remember that she was in the mall food court, eating with her best friend, Colleen Douglas. And to realize that Colleen was referring to the french fries that she'd barely touched.

"Uh, yeah, sure." Gabrielle pushed the triangular box of shoestring fries toward her friend. She didn't know why she'd ordered them in the first place: she was too miserable to eat. She drew a long sip of Diet Coke through her straw. At least this was moist and cool, made her stomach feel better. A little.

"What's wrong, Gabby?" Colleen was now more interested in her than the fries.

"I didn't say anything was wrong."

"Didn't have to. It's all over your face. You look as if Ryan dumped you all over again."

Gabrielle shot her a furious look. "I told you not to mention his name, ever."

"Sorry. But you do look really miserable. Why? Spit it out."

Gabrielle looked around the crowded food court without seeing it, then, as though overwhelmed by life itself, she buried her face in her arms on the table. She knew she was being overly dramatic, but she couldn't help it. Everything, it seemed, was a big deal. Everything seemed so . . .

Dark.

"I see no future," she said, her voice muffled in the sleeves of her sweatshirt.

"What do you mean?"

Gabrielle sat back up and tried to clear her head, reorganize her thoughts, find the right words so that her friend would understand exactly what she meant. "I've been thinking lately about that five-year thing Ms. Dubois was talking about in class the other day."

"Oh, you mean writing an essay about how you see yourself five years from now?"

"Yeah. Well, do you know what I see? Totally nothing."

"That's why you're miserable? Why you're acting like Ryan dumped you all over –"

"Hey, I said not to mention him."

"Sorry." Both of Colleen's hands shot up, palms out. "Anyway, I still don't get your problem."

"There's nothing I want to be in five years. There's nothing I want to do. I don't want to go to college. I'm totally sick of studying, you know? I don't have any definite dream, goal, direction. Nothing. I'm actually scared of the future. I don't know what to do with my life. What to be. I certainly don't want to be a housewife – how boring! – and push out babies for the rest of my life. Not that anyone would want to marry me anyway. I couldn't keep what's his name more than a month."

"Ryan."

Gabrielle glared at her.

"What is your goal, then?" Colleen added quickly.

"Haven't you been listening? I have none. I have nothing."

"I thought you wanted to be a doctor."

"My dad wants me to be a doctor – as if I'm smart enough. He's in denial."

"Well, then, maybe a nurse."

"Just because I like 'ER,' it doesn't mean I want to be in the med. profession. I mean, the sight of roadkill makes me hurl."

"You could backpack across Europe or something until you make up your mind."

"I couldn't care less about that. Sounds too lonely and too – oh, I don't know – risky. Stranger in a strange land sort of thing." She sighed, discouraged.

"Maybe you need a fortune teller or something."

"What?"

"You know, someone who can tell your future."

"Hey, not a bad idea. Know where I can find one?"

Colleen shook her head. "I've seen some ads for occult shops downtown, but you don't want to be going down there. These places aren't exactly in the best neighborhoods."

Gabrielle grabbed her purse from the table and shot to her feet. "Never mind that. Come on!"

"Oh, Gabby, you don't –"

But Gabrielle was already halfway out of the food court, her mind made up. She hoped she wouldn't need an appointment.

Hazy with burning incense of an indeterminate aroma and smelling ancient and dusty like an attic, the shop, called the Golden Unicorn, was typical with a mystical theme. But the fortune teller, who parted Sixties-style love beads to greet the girls from a back room, wasn't. Gabrielle had expected a middle-aged woman, complete with shawl, tent-like floral dress, maybe a silk kerchief on her head, tons of makeup and clanging jewelry – not a man who reminded her of Mr. Clean. This man was somewhere in his thirties, and he had his head shaved and one ear adorned with a golden hoop. Instead of being dressed solely in white like the icon of the cleaning product, however, he was in black. He smiled and bowed at the girls.

He's a fake! Gabrielle thought immediately. Anybody who shaved his head couldn't be for real. But since she was already in the shop, she couldn't leave gracefully. After all, what could she say? "I'm just browsing."

"How may I be of service to you pretty ladies?" the man asked. He had a voice as deep as some of those actors in old horror movies – and just as creepy.

Maybe I should leave anyway, Gabrielle thought. Who cares if I look like an idiot? But Colleen spoke up before she could respond.

"She wants her fortune read."

The man focused on Gabrielle, his smile widening. His eyes, she noticed, were almost black, the pupil and iris indistinguishable. Knowing she could easily lose herself in them, she looked away.

He said, "Tarot cards, palms, tea leaves, or the globe?"

"Uh . . ." She hadn't expected multiple choices. "Which is the cheapest?" The instant the words were out, she wanted to retract them. She couldn't believe it: she had sounded just like her father.

"The globe," the bald man in black answered.

Gabrielle nodded her assent. The man then led her to the back room, pushing aside the beads. Colleen started to follow, but the man turned around and stopped her. "The room fits only two at a time. Of course, if you wish to have your fortune told as well, I shall get to you as soon as I'm finished with this young lady."

He was polite yet firm. A momentarily discomposed Colleen had no choice but to retreat to the front of the shop and browse aimlessly at the collections of pewter jewelry, crystals, scented candles, books, and posters of wizards and dragons.

The back room, Gabrielle saw, consisted of only a table and two folding chairs, the former covered with black velvet cloth. This room indeed was too small to accommodate more than two people. The smell of an incense stick (frankincense? sandalwood?) burning in a banana-shaped holder on a shelf behind the table was stronger in here because of the confined space. Beyond was another room, this one with a real door instead of beads. Bathroom? The bald man's living quarters?

The man gestured for her to sit at the table. Once she was seated, he turned to the shelf and took down a crystal ball. Holding it in both hands, he set it down carefully in the middle of the table, as though it was as valuable as a Fabergé egg.

Fake! Gabrielle thought again. What am I doing here? Why do I care what he would think if I bolted? I don't know this man.

Yet they discussed price, and she pulled the required amount from her purse. "I want to know what I'll be doing five years from now," she said.

After tucking the money into the pocket of his black pants, he peered into the globe. It was clear glass, not crystal, Gabrielle was certain. There was nothing within the sphere except maybe a few milky swirls. However, the more Gabrielle stared into the ball, she saw, or thought she saw, the swirls move.

The man seemed to be seeing more, though, for he was soon frowning, seemingly with confusion, concern, unease. But when he looked up, the frown was gone, replaced by what looked like a controlled expression, a poor attempt to appear neutral.

"What?" She hadn't liked the frown, and she certainly didn't like the mask she was seeing now.

"I'm afraid I'm not receiving anything today," he said. "It happens now and then, you must understand. I'm sorry."

He's lying, Gabrielle thought. "You don't see anything at all?"

"I'm sorry," he repeated.

"Well, I want my money back."

"Of course." He pulled the bills from his pocket and slid them toward her.

She didn't like that either. So quick, so smooth – it was as if he couldn't wait for her to leave.

"Wasn't there anything at all?" she asked again when she was at the beaded entrance, the money in her hand.

She wasn't sure if she'd heard him right – his reply was too low, only to himself – but she swore he had said, "Only . . . darkness."

Gabrielle didn't let herself say anything until she and Colleen were at Colleen's house.

"I have *no* future!" she wailed once they were in the privacy of Colleen's room.

"What do you mean? What did the man say?"

"He couldn't see anything. You don't have to be a brainiac to know what that means. He saw nothing because there *was* nothing. I'm going to be *dead* in five years, Colleen!"

"Oh, come on, Gabby." Colleen pshawed. "That fortune teller was a fake. Couldn't you tell?"

"What am I going to do? I'm doomed."

"Don't talk like that. You sound like my dad when he got laid off. Now all he does is hang around the house and drink."

"Well, I *am* doomed," Gabrielle insisted. If there was only darkness in her future, what was the sense of doing anything? Maybe she should take up drinking too – and smoking, while she was at it.

"I don't like this," Colleen said as she watched Gabrielle stare up at the ceiling from a death-like position on the bed. "It's as if . . . as if you're giving up."

But Gabrielle wasn't giving up – not quite. She was thinking. Thinking hard. Hadn't Colleen mentioned, maybe years back, something about having an aunt who was a witch? Maybe someone like that, someone with spells and potions, could save her.

"Don't you have an aunt who dabbles in black magic, Colleen?"

"Oh, let's not go there."

Gabrielle sat up. "When we were kids, you used to talk about her. Is she still alive?"

"Yeah, she's still alive, but –"

"Is she still into witchcraft?"

"Yes, but she's . . ." Colleen crossed her eyes and twirled an index finger against her temple.

"Fix me up with her."

Colleen looked at Gabrielle as though she were wondering if she was as crazy as her aunt. "What on earth for?"

"Maybe she can give me an amulet or something to help me. Right now, I'll do anything."

Aunt Matty looked like a sweet, plump grandmother, not like a witch at all. But then, the fortune teller wasn't what Gabrielle had expected either. Aunt Matty graciously accepted her into her parlor, as one would accept a guest for a social chat, and urged Gabrielle to pour out her troubles as she poured tea into three tiny cups (the third for Colleen, who this time was allowed to be included).

It was easy for Gabrielle to express her concerns with Aunt Matty. The woman was all warm and fuzzy, truly the grandmother from children's books who made cookies and hot cocoa. After Gabrielle was finished speaking, Aunt Matty was quiet with thought for a long moment.

"So what you're saying is that you're afraid of the future," the woman said slowly, to make sure she had it right.

"I guess that's it," Gabrielle agreed, nodding. "I don't think I even *have* a future."

"And you want me to . . . ?"

"Help me somehow."

"Hmmm. Well, I could put together a pouch of garlic, pulverized mandrake roots, bulls' testicles, and other ingredients, which should help. If you carry this, keep it on your person, it will protect you."

Gabrielle glanced at Colleen in time to catch her rolling her eyes. Back at the woman: "How much will it cost?"

"Oh, not a thing, dear." She dismissed her with a don't-be-silly laugh. "You're my niece's dearest friend. For you, it will be a gift."

"Why, thank you."

"But remember" – Aunt Matty leaned forward and spoke in a cautionary voice – "whenever you feel you are in the presence of danger, you most hold this pouch close to your heart, spin seven times to the right, seven more times to your left, then walk backward thirteen steps. While you do this, you must keep your eyes closed and imagine the brightest, whitest light possible. Do you understand?"

"I think so," Gabrielle replied uncertainly. "But how will this help if danger comes without warning?"

Aunt Matty sat back with an expression of regret. "I'm afraid it can't. The only advice I can give you, dear, is to always be on the alert, to heed every sign you see, look for omens, treat every day as though it is your last. Let your horoscope guide you. Better yet, consult an astrologer. Do everything you can, dear, to protect yourself."

Gabrielle looked over at her friend again. Colleen's eyes seemed to be stuck in a heavenward position.

♉

"I am so embarrassed!" Colleen declared fifteen minutes later, after they had traveled in silence to Gabrielle's house.

Gabrielle immediately located her parents' morning newspaper and opened it to the horoscopes. "Why? She seems very nice," she said distractedly as she zeroed in on Aries, her sign.

"She's a flake. Certainly you're not going to be carrying a smelly pouch with you for the rest of your life!"

"Today you won't be thinking clearly," Gabrielle read without answering. "Don't take anything out of context or be undiplomatic when dealing with others. Physical activity will help alleviate stress."

"What are you doing?"

"What does it look like? Your aunt told me to use the horoscope as a guide."

Her friend was speechless for a moment, then she exploded. "What am I going to do with you, Gabby! You're taking this future thing way out of control. Why can't you just be cool? Let things happen?"

"My future is dark. If I don't do anything, I might be dead in five years – or just a big, fat nothing. Whatever is ahead of me, it's not good. So I've got to protect myself. Why is that so hard to understand?"

Colleen dramatically inhaled, exhaled, then muttered something Gabrielle couldn't catch.

"What was that?"

"I said," Colleen repeated slowly, clearly, as one would when speaking to a hearing-impaired person, "Aunt Matty isn't the only flake in my life now."

♋

"My horoscope today said carelessness could result in an accident," Gabrielle told her friend a week later, as they were browsing through the mall.

"I'm not listening," Colleen said, keeping her face straight ahead. A rack of jeans at Old Navy had caught her attention.

Gabrielle followed her into the store. "I have my pouch from your aunt with me, though. So I should be safe, right?"

Her friend, too busy inspecting a pair of low-rise jeans, didn't answer.

"But you were right about it being smelly. It stinks like a cow patch," Gabrielle went on, although she knew Colleen was ignoring her because she was sick of talking about this. "It doesn't smell as bad as it used to, though. Do you think when it stops smelling, it'll stop working? Your aunt Matty never did say if I should have the pouch replaced."

"Too bad I have an outie," Colleen said, mostly to herself.

"What?"

"I'm wondering if it's too gross to wear low-rise with an outie belly button."

"Oh. Uh, that's your decision. I'm hungry. I'm going to the food court."

"Me too. I'll decide later." Colleen put the jeans back and walked alongside Gabrielle toward the other end of the mall. They stopped at almost every store, barely paying attention to the walkway. They even peered down over the waist-high banisters at the shops on the ground floor far beneath them. Christmas was more than six weeks away, yet the mall was already festively decorated with tinsel, wreaths, and colorful lights. There was so much to see, so many stores with holiday sales.

"Do you realize what you just did?" Colleen suddenly said, looking back.

"What?" Curious, Gabrielle followed her friend's gaze.

A man was on a tall stepladder, adorning the top of Sears' entrance with lights. Gabrielle still didn't understand.

"You walked right *under* that ladder," Colleen explained. "That's bad luck, if you're superstitious."

Gabrielle suddenly felt cold all over, her heart and lungs locking up. "This . . . this was exactly what my horoscope warned me about. It told me that if I was careless, an accident would happen."

"Yeah, well, come on. Do you want to share an order of onion rings?"

Ignoring her, Gabrielle took the small, odorous pouch from her purse and pressed it close to her heart. She closed her eyes and then tried to fill her mind with the brightest, whitest light.

"Gabby, what are you doing?"

"Sh. I'm doing what your aunt told me." She began spinning to her right. Or was it supposed to be her left first?

"I told you, my aunt's a nutcase."

It was so hard to count seven revolutions while keeping an image of white, heavenly light in her mind. But when she finished (she hoped she'd done seven, not six or eight), she started her second series of spins, this time turning to her left.

"Gabby, people are staring!" Colleen hissed.

"I have to do this to protect myself. To protect . . . my . . . future," she said as she counted, as she concentrated.

When she stopped, she found herself a little dizzy. Now what? Oh yes, she had to walk backward thirteen steps while still clutching the pouch. One . . . two . . . three . . .

"I don't believe this! Gabby, stop it! I mean it!"

Four . . . five . . .

White lights. Bright lights. This was the hardest part, keeping the light in her mind as she counted. She made herself think of glowing angels, halos, heaven.

Six . . . seven . . .

"Gabby!" her friend screamed.

The rest seemed to happen in slow motion. Gabrielle found herself falling backward into empty air. Strangely, she didn't panic, only felt somewhat surprised, stunned. She heard her friend scream, heard strangers scream a million miles away. She felt like Alice falling down the rabbit hole to another world. Clutching the pouch tighter to her chest, she braced herself for the inevitable.

Darkness.

In Your Dreams

Mark A. Garland

T.J. was having a nightmare. It was the kind of thing that happened now and then, happened to everyone, right? Sometimes T.J.'s nightmares were just a lot of wild, ridiculous, upside-down craziness; sometimes they were short and intense; sometimes they came and went through the night; and sometimes they repeated, night after night or week after week.

The important thing with a nightmare was that when you woke up and realized that it was only a dream, that none of it had really happened, you could deal with it. You could take a deep breath, get up, go to the bathroom, and go back to sleep and hope the nightmare wouldn't come right back. Unless it was one of those nightmares that gets interrupted by the alarm, so you get out of bed all ragged and shaky, and you end up going to school actually eager to start listening to your first-period English teacher.

Then there's the kind of nightmare T.J. was having – the kind of nightmare you got only once in a while but never forgot. The kind with no wacky flaws, with a beginning, a middle, and an end; the kind that can ruin your life if you let it, because it seems absolutely real.

T.J. hated those. Like the one where everyone kept telling him that while he was a nice kid and they liked having him around and chatting and all, the trouble was that he'd been killed in a terrible accident, and why couldn't he just admit that and go on to "the next world" like a good little dead kid. "I don't feel dead," he'd tell everyone. But no one seemed to think that mattered. Then they'd take him to the scene of the accident and it was suddenly all too real, and he felt really, really dead.

This dream was like that, only he was apparently really alive and doing very well. He'd got up that morning and gone to school, managed to stay awake through first period, managed to stay out of the way of Robert B., the most notable of several missing-link types – a guy who usually slept in his logo clothes and skipped a lot of school and had a little supply-and-demand illegal-substance business on the side, a guy who liked to show people like T.J. a bad time. Then he'd run into Jessica Berry in the hall on his way to second period. Smashed right into her. She was wearing jeans tight enough to find the slightest flaw in any other girl's figure and a black stretch-knit, sleeveless top with the slogan "10% Angel, 90% Yours" printed in white letters across the front. T.J. couldn't take his eyes off the zeros. Until she paused, looked right at him, and said, "Hi, T.J." No scolding, no swearing. No ice.

He looked up at her perfect smile, her incredible dark eyes, the cascade of reddish-blond hair that fell about her. Jessica was beyond even his dreams, and T.J. had long accepted the idea that he would never, ever have a chance with a girl like that – even if he'd been "someone," which he was not.

"Hi," T.J. squeaked.

Jessica leaned toward him. "You know what I heard about you?"

She was still smiling, white teeth and high cheeks, head tipped slightly to one side, eyes blinking, cute as hell. How bad could it be? He managed a swallow. "What?"

"I heard that where you used to go to school, you had, like, twenty girlfriends. Maybe more."

"I did?" T.J. stammered, wondering where such a rumor had got started – and how he might someday thank that person.

Jessica's lips formed a mind-bending pout. "Didn't you?"

T.J. had never been popular – or good-looking, or self-confident – even before his parents had split up. His father had left for good a few years ago, and he and his mother had moved around a lot, first to L.A., then to Minnesota, then to upstate New York, where she'd finally found a decent job. Nothing much had gone right along the way, or since, as far as T.J. was concerned. He'd taken to hiding inside himself – or at least inside the house, if not in his room – and keeping everyone else out. But it was easy, because doing that seemed to come naturally to him, and because everybody seemed naturally to avoid him at this new school anyway. Especially the girls. It bothered him sometimes, and lately more than ever, but never as much as it bothered his mother, who was becoming obsessed with the idea of getting him out of the house and finding him new friends. It wasn't that T.J. didn't want to fit in; it was just that trying to fit in, trying to find his place, had never quite worked for him. And he knew that nothing he said or did was going to work for him now. Still, for some reason, he had a terrible desire to try. He took a deep breath. "Okay," he said. "How did you find out?"

"I just know everything."

It might be true, T.J. thought. Or it didn't matter. What mattered was that she was still smiling at him. He needed to say something else now, didn't he? Something real – nothing about the weather. He didn't really know a thing about her, but he knew something about himself. "I don't have very many friends in this school yet," he said. "How do you know my name?"

"Same as above. You going out with anyone?"

T.J. shuffled his feet. "Um, no . . . not . . . I . . . not right now."

Two other girls – both gorgeous friends of Jessica's – came by. One was rather short, almost tiny, and had straight, dark shoulder-length hair and the kind of complexion that always made her look like she had a perfect tan. T.J. was pretty sure her name was Ria. The other one was Courtney, a tall girl who looked, dressed, and acted very much like Jessica, except for the incredibly blonde hair, which turned into a basketful of loose curls around her shoulders. They pulled Jessica aside and began whispering, then the bell toned and the three of them snickered in harmony. Suddenly the others were gone, but Jessica was not. "I'm going that way," she said, waving an armful of books in one direction.

"Okay, sure," T.J. said, even though he wasn't sure about anything. They walked together and talked, and things went very, very well. He rode her bus home and sat next to her, and he walked her to her house and kissed her. Several times. By the time they said good-bye, they were going together.

He wasn't sure how he'd got home, but that didn't matter. What mattered was that a typically colorless, hopeless day at his new school had turned into the best day of his entire life, just like that.

T.J. called Jessica when he got home, and they talked for another two hours. She liked the same movies he did, some of the same TV shows, some of the same games. They'd both got driver's permits recently, and they both wanted their mothers to let them start driving. The only bump in the road was her love of hip-hop, which he couldn't stand. T.J. liked West Coast alternative rock. But he'd been to the West Coast and Jessica never had, so he didn't mind, even though Jessica seemed to think the whole music issue was pretty important.

T.J.'s mother finally made him get off the phone and go to sleep. When he woke up the next morning, he practically leaped out of bed.

His mother had cereal and milk out on the table for him when he came downstairs and headed into the kitchen. He ate only a little. He couldn't sit still. "Thanks," he said, "but I've got to get to school."

"What's going on?" his mother asked, with an overly sly smile. "You're acting kind of weird."

"There's this girl in school," he said, then he paused, trying to think of something to add.

His mother looked as if she'd seen a vision. "I can't believe it," she said, then she seemed to collect herself. "I mean, I hope she's nice."

"Believe me," T.J. said, nodding furiously, "she's nice."

She let him go. He couldn't wait to get off the bus at school. When he got inside and saw Jessica in the hallway near her locker, his heart started racing. He tried to look calm. He walked up and said hi.

Jessica was with the same two girls T.J. had met the day before. All three of them looked at him, then shrugged.

"Yeah, hi," Jessica said.

The tall blonde, Courtney, managed a deliberate frown, while the dark-haired girl actually winced. Then the three of them turned and walked away. Cold. Just like that.

In that instant, as he watched Jessica's consummate backside strut off into the annals of high-school history, T.J. began to question the reality off all that had happened. He breathed a ragged sigh as the full truth of the matter came to him in a dizzying rush. "It was all a . . . a dream," he said out loud. He felt something turning into thick, heavy knots in his chest. "No," he muttered. "It was a nightmare."

The rest of the day seemed normal enough. T.J. handed in all his homework, blew right through a science test, then slept in study hall. During lunch, he managed to find the perfect table – it was only half full and held nobody he thought might bother him or throw things at him, or get him talking and then trick him into saying something dumb or revealing. He'd been down those roads before, which was another reason he liked to keep to himself these days. Why take chances? Jessica sat across the cafeteria, eating light, talking continuously with a tableful of other girls and a couple of truly fortunate boys.

T.J. shook his head. In your dreams, he thought. He finished eating, got up and dumped his tray, then rambled past Jessica's table on the way back.

She looked up and caught him staring. She made a snotty face. "What?" she asked.

"Um, nothing. I was just –" Dreaming, he almost said, but he didn't.

"Hey, Jess is in love with you!" Ria, the dark-haired girl taunted, really loud.

"Oh, me too, me too!" Courtney howled. Everyone at the table laughed.

Those girls play a lot of games, T.J. thought. They can afford to. He started walking away.

"Guess *that* scared him off," he heard another girl say.

"Just as well," Jessica said, her voice unmistakable. "He hates our music."

That took a second to register, but when it did, T.J. nearly froze. He fought the urge to turn around and instead kept walking, kept steady until he was able to sit back down. How could she know? he wondered. But even as the question swirled through his mind, he knew there was only one possible, yet utterly impossible, answer.

T.J. was awake, wide awake, even though he'd been in bed for hours. He'd sometimes wondered whether the people he encountered in his dreams were *really* in his dreams. Or was he in theirs? He'd even asked his mother about it once. "I guess everyone thinks about that at one time or another," she'd said in her best "there, there" voice. "Some people imagine all kinds of things – that we have these spiritual personalities that leave our bodies at night and mingle on some kind of astral plane, or that our dreams are like ESP, flashbacks from past lives. *National Enquirer* stuff."

It had all sounded pretty foolish at the time, but he didn't think so now. By morning he felt awful, and he hadn't slept at all. His stomach felt sour, but he couldn't tell if that was from lack of sleep or worrying about what might be going on. He ate toast and thought about playing sick, staying home. No, he couldn't do that either. He had to know more. He had to find out, somehow – that was the one thing that lying awake all night had made him realize.

He had a rough morning at school. He couldn't think straight enough to do well in class, and he saw no sign of Jessica, even though he went out of his way to look for her. He spent the afternoon thinking about nothing else – until the end of last period, when everyone headed for the bus lineup and he saw his chance. T.J. knew what bus Jessica took, and he didn't really care if he missed his own. He just knew he had to talk to her. It was possible she had found out about the music some other way, but he didn't see how. No matter how he stacked things up, he kept coming back to the same inescapable truth: she had been there, really there, in his dream.

He reached Jessica's bus just as she did. She wasn't alone, of course – Courtney was with her. They were huddled together, talking. T.J. took a breath and held it, knowing that when he exhaled, he would say something and there would be no turning back. He'd make a complete fool out of himself, unless . . .

Unless he was right.

"I need to talk to you a minute," he said, biting his lower lip as he waited for any kind of reply.

Jessica looked at him with that perfect face and didn't smile. Instead, she seemed quite concerned, or perhaps perplexed.

"Why? About what?" she asked, serious as science.

"Just . . . just something, but it's important," T.J. said.

Jessica shrugged at the other girl and got a look in return that was heaped with meaning, though T.J. couldn't begin to imagine what the message was.

"Okay, but hurry up," Jessica said, taking a few steps toward the grass at the edge of the sidewalk. T.J. quickly followed, thinking things were going much too well. She stopped on the grass and glared at him. "Well?"

T.J. had decided this would be like going swimming in cold water: you could wade in slow and let the water creep up your body inch by icy inch, or you could just dive in and get it over with. "Have you ever . . . dreamed about me?"

Her fiery glare turned to ice. "No. Never."

"You sure? Two nights ago, maybe?"

She seemed to drop any notion of argument instantly. She looked back over her shoulder at her friend and shook her head. The other girl winced. Then Jessica turned to T.J. again, intensely focused. "This is a bunch of garbage," she said. "You're some kind of weirdo. Go home and play with yourself."

T.J. was determined. "I tried that. It doesn't help."

"You don't know what you're talking about."

T.J. had never seen Jessica so agitated. He'd touched something raw, and he knew it, just as he knew he couldn't let it go, not now. "But I *do* know, and so do you. How did you do that? What's happening to me at night – to us?"

Courtney stood close behind her now, listening in on the conversation and apparently at least as disturbed as Jessica. "How does he know?" she asked.

"He doesn't. I mean, he can't." Jessica looked off toward the school, toward the distance. "Can he?"

"Not if he knows what's good for him," Courtney said. Then she glared at T.J. "Got it?" she asked.

Jessica's eyes focused again, and she leaned close to T.J.'s face. "You got it?" she repeated. "You're just losing your mind, if you ever had one. Get help." Then she and Courtney whirled and headed for the bus.

"But I do know!" T.J. called after them. "What's wrong? Why won't you –"

They were gone. T.J. heard diesel engines starting, noticed the sidewalk thinning out. He turned and ran for his own bus and made it just in time.

When he got home, he looked up Jessica's number in the phone book and couldn't help noticing it was the same number she'd given him in his dream – or *their* dream. He tried calling her all evening. Someone claiming to be Jessica's mother in a voice that sounded a lot like Jessica's, only lower and a bit strained, kept telling him she wasn't home.

Finally he went to bed, completely exhausted yet afraid to fall asleep, to dream. But he couldn't help it and faded out in just a few seconds. He hardly remembered getting up the next morning, talking with his mother about nothing – the weather – and taking the bus to school. After homeroom, he headed toward his first-period class and almost at once realized he was being followed down the hallway by Jessica and her friends Courtney and Ria. They were a few paces back, working their way through the densely crowded hallway, but he could sense them closing, and he had an ominous feeling that no good would come of it. Just as he was about to turn and confront them, he felt hands grab hold of him – of his pants, to be precise. The hands yanked, like a magician snapping a tablecloth from under plates and glasses. His jeans and his boxers were suddenly gathered around his ankles, and he took half a step and fell flat on his face.

T.J. looked up from the floor as he rolled over, hands between his legs. Not everyone had stopped to stare, but the crowd was large enough, and everyone in it was hysterical. Jessica and her friends were nowhere to be seen. He felt an urge to scream, but some part of his mind had decided he'd already gained enough attention. He got up, pulled his pants up, and picked up his books and papers, all of which took long enough to make him late for class.

"It's a long story," he said when the teacher, Ms. Grimwald, asked him for an explanation. She was the sort of teacher who had probably been born without a sense of humor and had made no effort to acquire one.

"Perhaps you'll write it all down for me while you're sitting in detention," she replied.

T.J. tried not to look at anyone all through class. He knew some of the other students had been there in the hallway and had told the ones who weren't. He felt sick to his stomach, and he felt cold, even though he had a T-shirt and a sweatshirt on. When class was over, he inched his way out into the hallway, checking to see if anyone hostile was around, then made his way toward math class. He'd got only halfway there when he began noticing the way everyone was looking at him. Staring. Like he'd grown an extra head. He stopped in the boy's lavatory, looked in the mirror, and gasped: he'd broken out in a rash of historic proportions. Countless bright red welts covered his face and neck – some large, some small, but all of them hideous. His ears had turned as red as Christmas bows, and he realized that his sweatshirt was soaked with giant rings of sweat at the armpits. About half a dozen boys had come into the lavatory, and they were all staring at him. He pushed past them, back out into the hallway. The instant he did, he had to pee. He had to pee *bad*.

He turned in frustration and headed back inside, but the others were all coming out, one by one. He waited and waited, then he dashed through the doorway to one of the urinals – arriving too late. He looked down and discovered that a very large wet spot had encompassed most of the front of his washed blue jeans. This all seemed so horrible that he found it suddenly hilarious. At least I don't have to go any more, he thought. On the other hand, he now felt seriously sick to his stomach. *Seriously.* No, he told himself. Don't do it! He had to get out, get away. He put his hand over his mouth and ran out into the hallway again, shoving curious onlookers out of his way as he went.

Until he ran headlong into the school principal, Ms. Warner, a short yet stately woman in her late fifties who always dressed as if she was having lunch with a senator. Today she had on a cream-colored dress with a matching vest and shoes. Nearly everything she wore had the same smart-looking lace pattern sewn or etched into it.

T.J. puked over all of it, even the shoes.

He took a breath, wiped his chin, and left Ms. Warner screaming as he made a dash toward the front door of the school, which was in sight at the end of the hallway. He was only a few yards from freedom when Jessica stepped out of the last classroom doorway and simply stuck her foot out. T.J. did a flying bellyflop and slid the last few feet, where he found Courtney and Ria standing on either side of the two main doors. They opened one door each and smiled. T.J. got up slowly and moved carefully past them, wary of attack.

"You're going to get expelled for this, for sure," Courtney said, grinning wildly.

"No," T.J. said. "I'm going to dig a deep hole and live in it."

"Go home, think about what you've learned, then forget it," Ria said as the girls closed the doors.

T.J. walked home, showered, changed. The rash was gone, but he couldn't stop shaking. He didn't say a word to his mother all evening. He went to bed wondering what he'd do in the morning, how he'd face the day. Why hadn't the school called? He wondered what his father would have done, but they'd never got to the point where T.J. knew him well enough to ask those kinds of questions. Not even in T.J.'s dreams . . .

He awoke still thinking about the same things. He didn't want to get out of bed, but the sheets were soaked with sweat. Then he noticed that the clothes he'd taken off the night before were not on the floor where he'd left them. Or where he *thought* he'd left them. T.J. took several long, deep breaths and got out of bed. He found his clothes, including the pants he'd soiled, but they were clean. In that instant, a cold gust of reality chilled him to the bone.

A nightmare. Of course! And he'd known that, hadn't he? He'd simply forgotten . . . somehow.

He felt nauseated as he sat on the edge of his bed. He decided to tell his mother he was sick and stay home to sulk. Jessica and her friends had tried to teach him a lesson, tried to scare the hell out of him. And it had worked.

He felt like a fool; he felt alone, more alone than he ever had before; and he felt scared. Most of all, he felt lost, as if nothing at all mattered any more. He had no one to turn to, to confide in – nothing to hope for. The closest he'd come to anything like success had turned out to be a dream that had turned out to be a nightmare that had become all too real. Which didn't make any sense. His whole life didn't make any sense. He found it easy to tell himself that this was never going to work – his trying to fit in, trying to make friends, trying to be happy. His mother was wrong: it wasn't worth the effort. There was a very good chance that he would never know anything but enemies and disappointment, or indifference at best. Bad luck. The universe just didn't care.

The truth of it all became a heavy, suffocating darkness that spread in his mind and seemed to swallow him up. But in the belly of the beast, there in the clutches of the dark end of living, he reasoned that now he had nothing left to lose. Or almost nothing. There wasn't anything anyone could do to him any more.

But only a heartbeat after that, his despair began to transform itself into a new sense of purpose and direction. And in his mind, he saw the only thing that might still matter, something that hadn't mattered in a very long time but had made all the difference to his mother. Like her, he'd been on the ropes through everything that had happened to him. *For too long.* And that was long enough, he thought. By afternoon, he'd decided he wanted to get them back.

When you spend the whole day thinking about a thing, you sometimes get a lot done, and by the end of the day, a couple of thoughts seemed reasonably certain to T.J. One, Jessica and her friends knew exactly what they were doing, and they'd been doing it for a while. Two, he didn't think they were aliens or witches or people from another dimension – although anything was possible – he thought they had just figured out how to manipulate the system. Or someone had shown them. Either way, T.J. figured that if they could do it – if they could get into his dreams and turn them into nightmares – then maybe he could do it too.

As he lay in bed that night, thinking about it, still trying to come up with a plan, he began to wonder if he'd ever fall asleep at all. But at some point, well into the night, both his problems began to benefit from the same attempted solution. T.J. decided to keep one thought clear in his mind, no matter what, and that thought was Jessica. He forced himself to concentrate on her, on everything about her. He held those images in his mind and kept everything else out, reasoning that if he fell asleep, it would be the only means of finding his way to her. The effort finally cleared his mind and paid off. All at once he was asleep, yet strangely . . . conscious.

T.J. found himself at the mall, walking along, following three girls, and he knew exactly who they were. He'd thought about this moment all day, about what he'd do if a moment like this arrived. He had some ideas. Dreams weren't exactly real, he'd reasoned, so maybe you didn't have to follow the rules of reality. Maybe you could make up rules as you went along.

The mall was huge, with big atriums and a two-story open food court. Trees had been planted under rows of skylights. They thrived, as did a sizable sparrow population.

T.J. decided that the sparrows needed to fly over Jessica, Courtney, and Ria – all the sparrows, several dozen – and that they should have a bad case of the runs.

He kept thinking, concentrating on the birds while following the girls, and the events began to occur exactly as he'd pictured them in his mind. Like squadrons of tactical fighters, the birds swooped over the girls and dropped their loads, wave after wave, making a gooey white-and-brown mess of their hair, their tops, and their arms as they began to wave them over their heads. The girls screamed, then ran. Ria started to get out ahead of the others, then she tripped and fell, and the others fell over her. When the three of them got up, Jessica's lip was bleeding, Courtney's beautiful curls were knotted about her head like a turban, and Ria seemed to have trouble standing on her left ankle. Nevertheless, they were all back at a dead run in just a few strides.

They arrived at the pool and fountains, where the food court joined three intersecting hallways. The birds flew by, circled around, and began another run. Courtney saw them coming and started pointing and screaming again. At the last instant, Jessica leaped up onto the stone rim of the pool and jumped off. The water was only about two feet deep, but she managed to get herself submerged completely. As the bombardment resumed, the other girls followed her lead. When they came up for air, the birds had gone, but a fantastic crowd had gathered. Standing at the front of them all, grinning for all he was worth and feeling like someone brand new, was T.J.

All three girls seemed to focus on him at once. Then suddenly, the dream was over.

T.J. heard the voices downstairs as he was getting dressed for school – girls' voices, talking with his mother. He had a bad feeling about that. He knew there'd be hell to pay for what he'd done, retribution of some kind, by day or by night – probably both. But he'd made up his mind that it wouldn't matter, that he'd just go to school and see what happened. Still, he was discovering, in the light of the next day, that he didn't feel quite so ready. And he had never thought he'd have to face the problem before he even got out of the house. He did, however, feel a sense of satisfaction that he thought just might carry him past any obstacle the day presented.

He went to the bathroom, brushed his teeth, took a deep breath, and headed downstairs. He found Jessica, Courtney, and Ria, all smiling and chatting with his mom, and another kid, a boy about T.J.'s age but about half again his size, most of it muscle. T.J. had seen him with the others once or twice before.

"Why didn't you tell me about your new friends?" his mother asked, clearly delighted by the visitors. "They seem very nice."

"This is Rick," Jessica said, her perfect smile beaming as she introduced the big kid. "He wanted to meet you."

T.J. nodded a greeting, but he didn't say a word.

"Aren't you going to say anything?" his mother prodded.

T.J. shook his head no.

"So we'd better get going, or we'll all be late for school," Courtney said.

"Have a good day," T.J.'s mother said, going to the door, opening it for the group, and sending him – T.J. was sure – to his doom. He thought about hiding behind his mother. In fact, he thought about a lot of things, like having nothing and everything to lose all at once, and whether he'd ever see his father again. He felt his heart begin to pound a little faster, felt fear working its grip around his airway, tightening. He extended a cold, utterly pale hand to take his lunch money from his mother, then followed the others outside and down the driveway. He knew that as soon as they were out of sight of the house, things would change. When they reached the corner, all four of the others formed a loose circle around T.J., and Jessica put her hand on his arm.

"That was pretty good last night," she said, wearing a fiendishly sly and immensely attractive look on her face. "We didn't know you had the talent."

"Talent?" he repeated, trying to stop shaking.

"Most of us discovered what we could do at a younger age than you did, but I guess everyone is different," Courtney said.

"You're one of us now," Ria said, while Rick reached out, grabbed T.J.'s hand, and shook it.

"Welcome," he said. "You've got a lot to learn, but Jessica will take care of that, and she can do it too."

"There are a few more of us," Jessica said. "You'll meet them. It'll be fun."

"Don't worry," Courtney added. "You'll fit right in."

She meant it too, T.J. realized. They all did.

"Say something," Jessica prodded. "Say anything."

T.J. swallowed. He did have questions, too many, but he had some answers too. Maybe enough. "I . . . I . . . I never dreamed –" He caught himself, and the others burst out laughing.

"Let's go," Ria said, "or we really will be late."

T.J. stood there, unable to move, as the others turned the corner. Jessica and Courtney snickered in harmony, then grabbed both his hands and took him in tow.

O Silent Knight of Cards

Ed Greenwood

The Golden Goblin burned down on a Saturday night.

Men and boys alike huddled in the chill night air in their hockey jackets, watching the roaring flames lick hungrily at the stars. Firemen shouted and trotted around with hoses. Some of the men from the bar down the street ran to help them, swearing in what sounded like delighted amazement – but everyone knew the place was doomed.

As the bystanders watched, something cracked amid a swirl of sparks, and the Golden Goblinhunter Games sign fell into the street, streaming flames. It darkened swiftly, the squatting goblin grinning from the heart of the fire as if the blaze just made it feel cozy.

"I always hated that sign," Ben said softly, as if to himself. No one answered.

Ben and his three friends stood together, a cluster of grim teens off by themselves, shifting from foot to foot in the cold.

Saturday night was their gaming night. On Saturdays, the store's back room – a drafty corner between the crazy array of plywood that was nailed over the old loading-bay door and the little cubicle that held a dangling lightbulb, a skewed mirror, a cracked toilet, and the mark on the wall where there'd once been a sink – was always theirs. Had been theirs for the past six years, blizzard or drought, holiday or whatever.

Simon broke his usual silence to say what they were all bitterly thinking. "*Now* what?"

There were several heavy sighs. Someone dug the toe of his boot into the mud, and someone else uttered the inevitable: "Wherever we go, it won't be the same."

"I don't want to lose this," Jack Clemens said fiercely, somewhat surprising the other three. Jack was the darkly handsome guy – the only one of them who could never be labeled a nerd. Girls just crawled all over him, and he could very easily have filled his Saturday nights with more of them, the way he did every other night of the week.

He scowled at the fire as the last recognizable bits of grinning goblin sank into flame-whirled ashes and added in a despairing snarl, "It'll all just fade away, unless we . . ."

"Unless we what?" Simon murmured.

"Say the rest, hey? You want us to *what*?" Al snapped.

Jack waved a hand that meant he didn't know what to say. Simon glared at him.

Large, strong, and angry Simon Bledsoe looked angrier than usual. He towered over the rest of them, his fists thrust into the pockets of his worn and torn leather jacket. It was a *real* bomber jacket, had been worn by an uncle who'd flown bombers in some long-ago war. He spat into a muddy pothole already full of firefighting water and growled furiously, "And it's effin' *poker* night too!"

Simon's folks were poor, and Simon was poorer – except when poker night came around, every fourth Saturday. Then the dungeons, dice, and cards with dragons and glowing rings on them were swept aside, the flickering tube was slapped until its crazy lines resolved themselves into the hockey game, everybody ate twice as much, and Simon won the money in everybody's pockets. Darn near every time, or so it seemed.

As if Simon's snarl had slapped them all awake, everybody sighed and started to move about restlessly, looking around at the men who were now drifting back toward the bar. The flames were dying, the smoke was getting thicker, the excitement was pretty much over – but the Goblin was still gone.

"So . . . any ideas?" Al peered at the others as if they'd personally failed him.

Al Jannath looked as thin as a signpost beside Simon's broad shoulders – impossibly thin, with a voice as sharp as his features. High, cutting, and supercilious, a voice that perfectly suited what he was: the sort of "mad scientist" nerd the rest of the school loved to hate. All Ears, everyone called him, because his ears were so big and stuck out so far. If someone didn't kill him after class someday, he'd probably get through university in two years and own half the town ten years after that.

Jack cleared his throat, made a helpless "hell, I don't know" gesture, and said nothing. Devilishly handsome Jack Clemens, with his grin and his wavy black hair. He looked like some stud on a movie screen – square jaw, sleek biceps, flat stomach, and a strut. *The* strut. He caught every eye, male and female, when he entered a room.

He whirled around now and looked almost pleadingly at Ben, who was gazing sadly into the flames and shaking his head slowly. Affable, smiling Ben Knight, a barrel of a guy who never seemed in a hurry and never wore anything above his belt but large, old, and shapeless sweaters. Not your average heir to the millions of a stock-market wizard.

Ben turned to see who'd moved, stared at Jack for a

moment, and then said suddenly, as if bursting through a wall of reluctance, "Let's go to my grandad's house! Mom and Dad are still off buying islands, but they'll be back two days from now to clear out all of his stuff so they can sell the place. He has some cool old cards! And there's beer!"

"Years-old beer? Yahoo, no thanks," Simon growled. "He died – what? – three months ago?"

"No, no, it wasn't Grandad's. He drank Scotch and stuff. No, some client sent a case of bribes to my dad – a new sort of beer he's importing – and I figured Mom'd freak if she found it sitting there in her spotless grand front hall, so I swiped it. Took it over to Grandad's last night. I'm staying there now."

"The old magician's haunted house?" Jack asked, remembering the old, dark mansion – turrets and widow's walk and all the rest of it – that sprawled along a dark, wooded ridge frowning down on a good stretch of town. "Talk about *creepy*! Why d'you want to live there?"

Ben shrugged. "I like it. And it's got a card table you wouldn't believe."

"Leather top? All old, chunky wood?" Al asked, sounding interested.

"Couldn't we just go to your mom and dad's instead?" Jack asked Ben. "And use that monster stereo?"

"And sit around on weird designer furniture, trying to play poker on a glass table lower than our knees?" Al snapped. "No thanks."

Ben grinned. "And tromp all our munchies into Mom's white carpet? And have her freak like she did last time? No way! It's Grandad's or someplace one of you guys can come up with."

Al waved a hand to forestall any other comments and asked, "This card table – it's in a special room done up for playing, like?"

Ben nodded. "With brass naked ladies holding lightbulbs over our heads, yet."

Jack and Simon exchanged glances, nodded, and Jack turned toward his car – low, gleaming curves and candy red, of course. Ben had the rich folks, but Jack's parents had bought him the sort of racing machine that drew girls like a giant magnet.

"Now *that*," he said over his shoulder, "I've gotta see. My parental units hired your grandad to do my sister's birthday party once. Alsimmer Knight, Conjurer and True Magicks. The girls all thought he was spooky. Gladia shouted at Mum about ruining her party afterward, while Simon and I ate all the cake that was left. But *I* thought he was great. 'O silent knight of cards,' he said, all grand and waving his hands, and the cards changed. I've never forgotten that."

"Me neither," Simon agreed.

Ben didn't say anything.

"I don't like it," Ben said again. His voice was still quiet, but they could all tell he was upset.

"But we *can't* play poker with Dire Dragon cards, or any of the rest of these either," Simon argued. "No suits, no numbered cards! It's *poker* night, remember?"

He pitched a Hurl Deadly Spell card across the table and followed it with an Elf Maiden Surprised, the one with the picture on it that still made Al blush. "I mean, *look* at these! Fun, yeah. But for poker? Get real!"

"Yeah," Al agreed. "Hand over that deck, Ben. C'mon!"

"No. Grandad said these cards were special," Ben protested, his hand still firm atop the worn deck of old Radiolamobile playing cards. "'Not for gambling, never for winning tricks. Too dangerous.' Those were his exact words. This was his Silent Knight deck – the one he used for his magic tricks."

"What's so magic – or dangerous – about a Radiolamobile? They went under, didn't they? They're just old cards," Jack said scornfully.

"*And* they're the only regular cards you've got," Simon added. "So make sure they haven't got any buzzers or other magic stunt stuff shuffled in with them, and then *deal*!"

Ben lifted his hand and looked down at the greasy old cards. He fanned them out with his forefingers, sighed, and protested quietly, "Grandad said never to use these. He showed me where he put them, in the box, and then told me never to 'just play cards' with them. *Three* times, he said that."

"Huh? When my dad says 'never, never, don't,' he knows I will," Jack told them, reaching out for the old cards. "He says things like that just to get me to look at things. 'To forbid is to lure,' he says."

Ben gave him a curious look. "That's just what my grandad used to say."

Jack grinned. "At my sister's party, my dad snuck into the back room, where he could watch your grandad's tricks. I bet he heard it then, thought it sounded good, and started saying it himself. He could never do those card tricks, though. I remember him trying and swearing all over the place."

He beckoned with his outstretched hand – and Ben looked at it, sighed, and put the deck of old cards into it.

"So what was a Radiolamobile, anyway?" Jack asked, looking down at a card. It was an eight of clubs that looked like any other well-used eight of clubs on one side and had the green, gold, and chrome Radiolamobile logo on the other. He turned over another – the ten of hearts – and then shrugged and started shuffling them.

"A car that died out because it wasn't as good as it claimed to be," Al guessed. "Like a card trick isn't real magic. People catch on, you know?"

Ben sighed, shrugged, and didn't say anything.

"What *is* this stuff?" Al asked suspiciously, holding up his beer mug to one of the brass ladies. The room wasn't just dim – it was dark. And this so-called beer . . .

"Old Innsmouth Horrid?" Jack suggested jokingly, raising his own mug in a mock toast. "Stop bitching and play!"

All Ears sat back with a sigh. "Not with this hand. I'm out." He pushed away some of the gold coins in front of him and said grudgingly, "Nicest chips I've ever played with."

Ben shrugged. "They were in the box with the cards. I'd never seen them before last week, but they look old. Pirate doubloons, maybe? I know Grandad used to play with men who owed him money. Playing for keeps, he called it."

"Huh," Al said, wiping foam from his mouth with the back of his hand. "Were any of them ever seen again?"

"Haw, haw," Jack said, throwing down his cards with an expression of helpless dismissal. "So can *you* deal me a better hand than Simon, hey?"

All Ears spread his hands. "I can't even deal myself a pair of anything, so don't expect miracles. Pass me another beer."

"Ho, ho," Simon said, looking up from where he'd been holding out his cards to compare with Ben's and reaching out to rake in the chips. "Not such a bad brew all of a sudden, is it?"

"It . . . grows on you," Al replied. "And spare me the 'like mold' comments and bad H. P. Lovecraft jokes, okay?"

"Aww," Jack and Ben said in mocking chorus as Simon raked the cards together.

He handed them to the mad scientist. "Deal away, Al, and make Handsome here happy."

"I think I'm the wrong gender to manage that," Al said, pushing his smudged glasses back up his nose. "But let's try for some better cards. For me, at least – he can have whatever's left over after that."

"Even that will probably be better than what I've seen so far this night," Jack said, leaning back in his chair to survey the dark, worn cave of a room. It was . . . cozy, that was it. Welcoming, despite the distant creakings – and the miles of gloomy stairs and frowning furniture they'd passed to get up here. Al was right too: the beer *did* grow on you. And not just the way all beer did. The flat, bitter taste was blah at first, but then . . .

He collected his cards, looked at them, and groaned. "*Al*!"

All Ears shrugged, sour-faced. "Don't look at me. Whatever's in your hand, mine's worse."

Jack rolled his eyes, then he spread his hands grandly and intoned, "O silent knight of cards!"

Ben looked up quickly. "Don't," he said flatly. "I . . . just don't."

The room seemed suddenly very warm and spicy – and then the peculiar smell was gone just as abruptly, and the cards in everyone's hands became as cold as ice.

Four startled faces glanced down at them, and eyebrows slowly rose all around the table.

Somebody said a very rude word, and someone else dropped his cards as if they were on fire and just stared at them.

"I thought we were playing poker with good old greasy, worn-out cards from some long-gone car company," Simon said slowly. "But it seems this silent knight, whoever he is, prefers tarot. Now *that's* a magic trick."

"Jumpin' holy ghost," Al said slowly and softly. Jack said something much shorter and nastier.

Everyone was looking at his cards now and holding them up to various brass ladies to see every last detail.

"Funniest tarot *I've* ever seen," Al said slowly. "The Loosed Hounds, Wind from the Tomb, the Silent Chancery – look at these pictures!"

"Yes," Ben said with distaste, putting his cards down. "Not very nice art."

"But good! It grabs you," Simon said, leaning forward to better catch the light, interest building in his voice. "The Toppled Turret, the Pointing Bone, Strange Spoor . . ." He brought a card close to his nose to scrutinize it in the dim light. "The Skull in the Well," he said wonderingly. "And there it is, in the bucket at the bottom. *Fantastic* art!"

Wordlessly, Al passed his hand to Simon, fanning out the cards and putting his finger on one particularly striking scene.

Simon peered at it. "Eyes in the Ruins," he read out. And then, more softly, he recited, "'No matter how she turned, the coldness of their regard touched her skin like skeletal fingers.'"

"They all have little verses like that," Jack put in, fanning out his own cards. "Here's the Unseen Guest. It tells us, 'By the time he saw what had come in when the door stood open, it was too late.' Huh. Sounds like a bad horror show."

"Cue organ chords," Al said, reaching for his beer. "Show Simon what else you've got. We're going to have to deal again, anyway – or find some new cards. Or maybe you'd better call on the knight again, Mr. Wizard!"

"He may not be able to help me now," Jack replied, holding up a card for Al to see. It depicted an armored knight striding through a moonlit hall, sword raised in gauntleted hands and visor open to reveal a skull grinning out at whoever was holding the card.

Al drew back his head as if Jack had made a threatening movement toward him, and then he thrust it forward again to study the card and quoted, "The Skeletal Knight. 'In the end, if steel not sunder, all that remains is walking bones.'"

"Let's see the rest of them," Simon said eagerly, holding out his hand. "These are . . . I've never seen anything like these before."

"I'll say," Jack agreed. "Here you go. The Missing Knife Found, the Lurking Watcher, the Thing in the Attic, and something called Shoqqa, God of Thirst."

Al lifted his mug. "Sounds like Lovecraft's stories. You know, Cthulhu?"

"Sounds like, yes, but I don't remember any Shoqqa," Jack replied.

"Hey, everyone and his girlfriend's maiden aunt once wrote Mythos stories and had a go at adding beasties with strange names," Al replied. "So it could be Cthulhu."

"Could be a lot of things," Simon said slowly, squaring up the cards. "They're tarot cards, though. It's the first time I've seen the Cups shown as inverted skulls atop winestems, with booze pouring out the eye sockets, but there you go. A little scary at first, but a cool trick to top all cool tricks." He shook his head in admiration and held out the deck. "Ben, we need another pack of cards. Don't lose these, though. I'd like to look at them again another time."

Ben took them. "I don't know about finding another full regular deck," he said slowly. "All the rest in the box were for pinochle – y'know, printed without the twos through eights of each suit – but I'll have another look through them. We could write numbers on some of the duplicate face cards, I guess." He got up, went to a shelf that was barely visible in the gloom behind him, and came back with a polished wooden box carved with elephant feet at all four corners. Its lid was a single slab of glossy green jade.

Jack whistled. "Your grandad wasn't hurting, was he? That's gotta be worth –"

"Nothing to him now," Ben replied with a shrug, flipping open the lid. "And it probably wasn't all that pricey back when he got it." He slid some cards out of a paper sleeve like the ones banks used to bind bills, turned them over, and froze.

"That's funny," he said very quietly, holding the cards up to the nearest light and fanning them. "I peeked at these last week, and . . . and . . ."

"What?" Simon asked, frowning, as he reached for his beer. "They were regular suit cards, you mean, and now they've all gone 'funny tarot'?"

Ben took out another deck and then another, and then he looked up and nodded wordlessly. His face was a little pale.

"Just like the deck Jack here . . . ah, changed?" Simon asked.

Ben looked down at the cards in his hand and nodded. "Looks like he changed all of them."

"Well," Al said firmly, "he'll just have to change them all back again. How'll we know what's high card? Does old Shoqqa outrank the Thing in the Attic?"

"Right, then," Jack said with a smile, rising to his feet and putting down his beer in one motion. "Ahem!"

"Uh, Jack," Ben said quickly, "I'm not so sure this is such a good –"

"Hey, now! The first magic I ever worked," Jack protested, "and you wanna spoil it. Maybe it works only once for each of us, but hey, this is fun! I've never been a card wizard before!" He grinned, spread his arms with a grand flourish, and intoned loudly, "O silent knight of cards!"

There was a moment of silence, as if everyone in the room was holding his breath. The cards grew icy in their hands.

Then, just outside of the room, someone laughed.

Everyone whirled to look at the open doorway, but the hallway was empty – just the strip of floor, its railing, and the open air of the huge high-ceilinged hall beyond.

"Who's there?" Al shouted, and his words echoed back off the hall ceiling. There was no reply. After a moment, Simon and Jack exchanged glances, then rushed to the door together and peered out.

Nothing. The passageway, the stairs down, and the hall below were all empty – and quiet, except for the boys' own anxious breathing. The front door was closed. After a moment, they went back in.

"Nobody there," Simon said, looking almost accusingly at Ben.

"The alarm system's the best," Ben told them quietly. "Nobody had been here before us, and nobody's got in downstairs while we've been playing or there'd be bells ringing all over the place."

"I sure heard that laugh, though. We all did," Jack snapped. And then he frowned. "Could it have been . . . your grandad's magic? Y'know, some sound effect to go with the cards changing?"

"Well?" Al asked, squinting at Ben. "Did it work? Did they change?"

Ben Knight spread his cards. "Oh, yes. They changed, all right," he said in a strange, rasping voice, and he flung them down on the table.

Looking pale and sick, he sprang up and almost ran out of the room, turning left toward the bathroom. His three friends exchanged looks and then peered at the top card, which was face up on the table.

It showed a wildly staring man, frozen in the act of toppling. He was clutching his throat, and his protruding tongue was a long, slimy, green thing with barbed ends – or perhaps it was sporting two tiny horns, like the head of a snail. It was entitled Death, and the inscription beneath it, in flowing script, announced, "Eventually one's thirst is only for life."

"I think he's gone to throw up," Jack hissed. "This is really creeping him ou –"

There was a loud double thud from the room next door, and then the bell-shiver of breaking glass. "Ben?" Al called, voice shrill in alarm. "Ben!"

Silence was the only reply. The three gamers looked at each other and then suddenly bolted for the door in unison. Jack was nearest, but Simon somehow got there first.

Ben Knight was lying on his back in front of the bathroom sink, a broken glass beside him and a steady stream of water still running from the tap. He was staring at the ceiling – and beyond. The tongue lolling out of his gaping mouth was a foot long or more, glistening green, and barbed at the end. Those tiny barbs curled and twisted – inquisitively, it seemed – and they were the only thing in that bathroom that moved.

Except for Simon, who was rising and backing away from the body so swiftly that he nearly took out Jack's teeth with his shoulder. "He's dead," Simon announced tersely. "He's not breathing, anyway."

"God!" Jack swore. "But that's . . . the cards couldn't have . . ."

"Couldn't they?" Simon snapped, heading for the stairs. "I saw a phone by the door. We'd better –"

"Oh, *no*," Al whispered, staring down at his hand. There was a card in it that hadn't been there before, and it was . . .

Jack swallowed and looked back into the gaming room, to make sure that the Death card was still on the table. It was.

But Albert Jannath was holding Death too. *Another* Death

card, identical to the first. He flung up a hand to his throat and threw the card away from him.

"No!" he shrieked, his voice rasping. "*No*!"

All Ears crashed past Jack and stumbled toward the stairs.

Simon stood like a post and let him go, not even turning when the despairing shriek rose, became a descending wail, and then ended with a very sudden thud on the floor of the entry hall three floors down. He was looking at the card that had suddenly appeared in his own hand. Jet-black back, with a green border of tiny crawling snakes intertwined . . .

"*Don't* turn it over," Jack snapped, and Simon saw that he too held a card. "O silent knight of cards!" he added quickly, flinging his arms wide. He looked as darkly handsome as always, like Dracula in some movie Simon hadn't seen yet, where he wore a leather jacket and got all the girls.

Jack's voice echoed in the high stairwell, and they both looked down at their cards.

Simon found himself staring at the black back of a Radiolamobile playing card no longer. Out of the white, round-cornered frame of the face of the card, the wildly staring, green-tongued man blazed up at him. That agonized face was . . . his own!

There was another face visible behind it, this one looking over the dying Simon's shoulder – a face that hadn't been on any of the other Death cards. It was an old, white-bearded face with glittering dark eyes and an eager grin. It was an older, bonier version of Ben Knight.

"Ah, I feel even stronger," said a dry, gloating voice in Simon's ear, and then it added a chuckle. "Young blood . . . so much energy, so much *life*! Ben and now young Jannath. The old spells are the good ones – yes, indeed."

As Jack started to shout – a hoarse shout that rose into a scream – Simon Bledsoe whirled around and ran as hard as he could at that voice, snatching out the knife he always wore inside his sleeve and thrusting desperately without looking.

He found nothing. Nothing but air. Magically, no banister or railing was at the top of the stairs to stop his fall, or even splinter before his charge.

A moment later, he found something – something very, very hard. It was the floor of the entry hall, already wet with Al's blood.

"Presto! No banister!" Alsimmer Knight's cold laughter rang out as Simon bounced helplessly, things breaking inside him. "Ah, well done, Grandson! You were always a fool, Ben – but a useful fool. How many times did I warn you not to play with those cards? Enough, it seems, to make them irresistible! Can you hear me, Ben? Can you *hear* me?"

A dry rattling sound followed, but Simon never knew if it was a reply.

The last thing he heard, as shattered bones burned and his slithering tongue rose up to choke him, was a loud, rolling laugh that gave way to the booming words "O silent knight of cards!"

Then the world was full of whirling cards, all black backs and . . . darkness.

In the Shadows

Michael Kelly

There was a monster under David's bed, hiding in the shadows. Not a monster like his father, but a monster all the same.

David lay in his too-small bed, in his too-small pajamas, in his too-small room, and trembled. He hated shadows. They were sly tricksters. That's why he kept the lights on. Shadows were dark and silent and mysterious, quietly creeping up on you when you least expected them. Like his father, David thought.

At first, when the shadows had made themselves known, he kept a flashlight by the bed. But that had been a mistake. When he switched it on, it threw harsh yellow light and black angular shadows around the room. He'd panicked. His room had tilted and David had dropped the flashlight. It had hit the floor, winked out, and rolled under the bed. It was still there, somewhere amid the dust and cobwebs. He didn't want to retrieve it.

So now he just lay in the dark room, night after night, telling himself that the whispers and rustlings he heard were just his imagination. But still he kept his bedroom light on. Otherwise the thing under his bed would scrabble out and eat him up. He was sure of it.

There was a soft knock at his bedroom door. David tensed.

Don't open the door, he thought. Don't open the door. Go away.

A whisper. "Davey? Are you awake?"

David didn't answer, hoping she'd think he was asleep.

Another short rap on the door. "Davey? Is that light still on?"

David groaned. He was fourteen – hell, almost fifteen – and she still called him Davey. Almost as if she never wanted him to grow up. His father, on the other hand, couldn't wait for him to grow up and become a man.

He heard the key slide into the lock. David gasped. She wasn't supposed to be up here after lights out. Father's orders. No bedtime visits. No stories, no tucking in. No outward displays of affection. How was he to grow into a man if he was pampered all the time?

The doorknob clicked. David watched it slowly turn, then he watched the door creak open.

His mother's tired face peeked into the bedroom. "Davey, my precious, you're still awake."

David sat up. "You have to leave, Mom. Quickly, before he gets home."

Softly. "I know, but it's payday. He's gone to the tavern. He'll be a little while longer." She stepped into his room, leaving the door ajar. She slipped the big brass key into her apron, then looked at him with her worrisome "let's fix it before your father finds out" look. At least it was better than his father's "this is going to hurt you more than it does me" look.

David glanced quickly to the open door, his heart racing like a caged canary. His mother had never before unlocked his bedroom door. She seemed not to notice how it yawned invitingly. Carefully, she tiptoed over to the bed, bent close to him. Her eyes were swollen and puffy, as if she'd been crying. She smiled weakly. David eyed the large brass key poking from her apron pocket. She followed his gaze, shushing him with a finger to his lips.

"He doesn't know I have the key, Davey. I found it in his dresser. Quickly now, turn out the lights before he gets home."

"But –"

"I know, sweetie. I know. But there are worse things than shadows. Am I right?"

David nodded.

"Good." She indicated the bell on David's night table. "Ring if you need anything: water, a bathroom trip."

Another dull nod.

"Very well." She bent, kissed his forehead. "I do love you, Davey. I do." She smoothed the hair from his forehead. "Things will get better soon. I promise." She straightened, turned to leave.

"Don't!" David said. "Don't go. Please stay. Just for a little while. Talk to me."

Her face drooped like warm putty. "You know I can't." She motioned over her shoulder. "If *he* catches me –"

"There'll be hell to pay." His father's voice cut into the room, a buzz saw through butter.

David's mother jumped. Her hands fluttered like mad moths in front of her. "I . . . I . . ."

"Shut your cake hole, woman."

David kept his head down, staring at the floor. His father's shadow loomed, stretching out like a dark ribbon of bone. David cowered, burrowed under his covers. The floorboards creaked and groaned as the lengthening shadow drew near.

David peeked over the covers. His father stood beside his mother, a grim smile creasing his face. He plucked the key from her apron and eyed it curiously, the smile widening.

"I see we've been busy while I've been gone," his father said. "While I've been at work – earning the money that keeps us in this house, that keeps food on the table and clothes on your back – you have been snooping around like a rat."

His mother, head down, said nothing, her hands twisting in the folds of the apron.

The shadow coiled and bunched, crawled slowly up his mother's legs like water on a drowning swimmer.

David's father leaned close, whispered to her with quiet menace. "I don't like rats."

She looked up, glanced at David. "Please, the boy –"

"Enough!" A large beefy hand flew up, gripped his mother's face, and squeezed. "Go set the table. I'm hungry." He shoved her, and she almost fell to floor. "I'll deal with you later."

David's mother gathered herself, stood, brushed and smoothed her wrinkled clothes.

"Go!"

With a fleeting glance at David, she slipped from the room.

The shadow turned, crawled up David's bed. David trembled, his teeth chattering.

"Ah," his father said. "The boy. Always the boy." His father's eyes flashed quicksilver. "I trust you had a good day at school?"

David nodded.

"That's good." His father took a step forward. "And how old are you, son?"

"F-fourteen," David answered.

"Fourteen." His father chuckled. "Almost a man. When I was fourteen, I was already working. I didn't have the luxury of school. Didn't have time for books and studies. Wasn't afraid some bogeyman was hiding under my bed. I had to work. And work makes you hard. You're soft, boy. You could use a little hard work. A little discipline."

David's father stepped over to the bed, his legs pressed against the side. The creeping black tide engulfed David, swallowed him in darkness. He flinched, drew back. His father bent, grabbed him by the front of his pajama shirt, and hauled him to a sitting position. Then he leaned in close. David's head swam, caught in the heady smell of grease and whiskey and tobacco that wafted off his father. His father was inches away, an indistinguishable form.

"Time for some discipline, boy."

David cringed. He wished his father would leave, go away.

A thump from under the bed. His father turned. A scratchy rattle and scuttling sound reached them.

"What was that, boy?"

David cringed, spoke in his squeaky mouse voice. "The monster, sir."

"Not this again. We've been through this already. That's why I locked your door – to make you a man. To prove to you that there's nothing in the room, boy – not in the closet, not under the bed. Just in your head." He jabbed David's forehead with his index finger. "In that thick, thick head."

With tears pooling in his eyes, David looked up at his father. "It's under the bed. In the shadows."

"Once and for all, I'll prove it to you," his father said. He bent down, peered under the bed.

David pulled his knees to his chest, hugging himself. His body shook. "Please, don't," he sputtered. "Th-that's not a good idea."

"Hush!" David's father said, kneeling. "Don't be a fool, boy." He leaned closer, his head almost completely under the bed. "What's this?" he asked, his hand snaking under too.

"Please, Father. Stop."

David's father pulled back. His hand was caught in some gauzy gray material that trailed away under the bed. He reached over with his free hand to try to pull it off, but that only made it worse. Now both hands were trapped. He thrashed and flailed at the sticky substance.

"Boy, I . . . I . . ."

David flinched at the guttural cry, waiting for his father's hand to strike him. He waited, but the yelp turned into a piteous wail.

"I need some help."

David rocked back and forth, back and forth. "I tried to warn you. You wouldn't listen."

"Son, I –" But the man's voice was cut off as something dark and hairy crawled from under the bed and gripped him in two pincer-like arms. He screamed in pain and terror. David had never heard anything like it issue from his father's mouth.

David rocked back and forth.

The thing turned, clutching David's squirming father, and stared at him with jeweled, faceted eyes. A black mouth gaped, saliva oozing from the maw. Then the mandibles clicked, as if it were trying to speak to David. David opened his mouth, trying to respond, but the creature scrambled under the bed, dragging his father with it.

Minutes later, David was still rocking back and forth, back and forth. "I tried to warn you. You wouldn't listen."

Muted sounds drifted up to him from under the bed: screams and moans, ripping and chewing and slurping. David continued to sit on the bed, rocking back and forth.

After the sounds had faded and the shadows had moved on, David leapt from the bed and sprinted for the open door.

Virtually Friends

Loren L. Barrett

When they arrived home, Jason's dad took the first and largest box from the car and headed downstairs.

"Where are you going, Dad?" Jason asked.

"To the basement, where I made space for it."

"But I thought I'd get to keep it in my room."

"What gave you that idea?"

"Uh, the fact that it's *my* computer."

"Just because Uncle Joe said it was for you doesn't mean I don't have a say about where it goes."

Jason stood in the hallway with his mouth open, hoping his father would notice the disappointment on his face. When his father ignored him, he muttered, "Okay. Whatever!"

That got his attention. "Look, Jason, you might feel all grown-up at seventeen, but you still live under my roof, understand?"

Jason's eyes swept the floor. "I understand." He sighed, then followed his father down into the basement.

In less than half an hour, Jason's dad had all of the pieces out of the boxes and in place, ready to go. Jason called his mother down for the big event.

"Okay, everyone," his father said, "here we go."

He pressed the power button, and all three of them watched as the computer started itself up, automatically loading all kinds of pre-installed software.

The messages on the screen seemed quite friendly.

Do you want to install your Internet access?

"Say yes," Jason said. "It came with three free months of online service."

"Oh, you know the lingo already, do you, son?" chided Jason's father.

Jason's dad clicked on the OK button, and after the computer logged on, it immediately asked for a user name. Jason pulled aside the keyboard and typed in his own name, but the computer told him that it had already been taken. So he typed "Jason007," and the online service provider welcomed him as a new user.

"Seems easy enough," noted his dad.

Do you wish to have parental controls?

"Yes, I think that might be a good idea," said Jason's dad, clicking on the Yes button.

Geez, thought Jason. His parents were already taking over his computer – probably not what Uncle Joe had had in mind.

"I've read a lot about the Internet lately, Jase. Lots of weird things happen to kids with unsupervised access. Parental controls don't seem like such a bad idea."

Jason sighed.

His father reached into one of the boxes. "See, there's even a manual in here called 'The Internet and Children.' Maybe you should read it."

Jason wanted to start surfing, not read the manual. He

wasn't a *child* any more, and it was only a big electronic box. He didn't know much about hacking, so he wasn't going to get into any trouble there. How could anyone get into difficulty using a computer, anyway?

"I'll read it later, Dad. I want to see how much information I can find for my next school project."

His father said nothing for a moment, as if he was considering Jason's intentions. "Sure, son, just don't stay on here all night, okay?"

"Okay, Dad."

Jason spent hours exploring the Internet, from local and international news to Web sites devoted to his favorite bands and movie stars. Jason also learned how to use a keyword search to find out about special things that interested him. After trying "monster movies" and "snowboarding," he typed in the words "naked women," just for the hell of it. Because his father had installed the parental controls, Jason expected a list of *National Geographic*–type sites, or even medical sites having to do with the human body. But to his amazement, hundreds of adult-oriented Web sites came up in descending order from most to least popular.

But that couldn't be right.

Jason had been there when his father had activated the parental controls. He'd seen him click the button.

Well, he wasn't about to tell his father that he was capable of entering X-rated sites – at least not until he had had the chance to show off the computer to a few of his friends.

He smiled from ear to ear.

"Jason, can you get off the Internet, please?" his mother yelled down the stairs. "I need to use the phone."

"Damn," Jason whispered under breath. "In a minute, Mom."

"Get off the line," she said again. "*Now*!"

"Getting off . . ."

That night, Jason lay awake in bed, thinking about the new computer and all its possibilities. It was as if a whole new world had opened up to him. As a result, he didn't fall asleep until the small hours, and in the morning, he was late getting out of bed.

"Come on, sleepyhead," his mother said from out in the hall.

"Huh?"

"Any longer and you'll miss the bus."

Jason tried to answer but couldn't. He coughed to clear his throat . . . and felt a sharp pain.

"Here, take your temperature, kid." She handed him a thermometer and stood there waiting. After a minute or so, the thermometer beeped and she looked at it.

"Uh, oh."

"What?"

"You're running a bit of a fever," she said. "It must be the start of the flu." She looked away, as if thinking. "You stay in bed. I have a few houses to show this morning, and then I'll be home for lunch. Drink lots and stay warm!"

Oh, great, thought Jason. He wanted to go and tell the world about his new computer, and here he was sick at home. But there was an upside to being sick now that there was a computer down in the basement.

Jason slept for all of another thirty minutes, then he dragged himself downstairs and turned on the computer. When he logged on, Jason realized that his father must have done something wrong with the parental controls because his e-mail box was jammed with letters from all sorts of places advertising sex, sex, sex.

A certain CindyLou wanted to know if he would like to see her undress in the girls' locker room, and a Doc Big asked if he wanted to be more of a man.

And on and on the letters went.

Wow!

Jason was thrilled, and he loved getting e-mail. Even though the letters were coming from advertisers for things he'd never use, at least someone out there knew he existed.

As he settled in to read the rest of his mail, a large white box appeared on the screen. At the top of the box, it said: "BlondeSue wants to chat with you. Will you accept?"

Jason didn't know what to do, so he ran his mouse over the box trying to get it to do something. Finally, a menu dropped and he was able to type words into it.

"Hello," said the name above his.

"Hello," typed Jason.

"I'm Sue, 16, blonde and have a great pair of legs. And U?"

Jason didn't know what to say. I mean, BlondeSue could be anyone, anywhere. She was a total stranger. Would Jason speak with a stranger he met at the variety store around the corner? Especially if she was a girl? The answer was definitely no, but there was something about the way the strange girl showed interest in Jason that excited him.

He wasn't the best-looking guy in the world, and this was the first time a girl had ever showed any real interest in him.

"Do U have a pic?" was the next message she typed.

"No," Jason answered.

Even if the scanner had been hooked up, he didn't know how to use it yet.

"This is my first time," Jason wrote.

"What's your name?" Sue asked.

"Jason."

"Shit," he said out loud, realizing he shouldn't have used his real name. Oh, well, too late now.

"Hi, Jason. And how old are you?"

"I'm 21."

Damn, he thought. Why did he lie? Would Sue have logged off if he had told her he had just turned seventeen?

But a lie or the truth, it was all very exciting. A total stranger of a teenage girl was interested in him! She thought he was twenty-one, and that was only a start. He could be any age he wanted, be any person he wanted. Who would ever know?

Jason spent the next twenty minutes chatting. It was all good clean fun, until she asked: "Can I have your phone number?"

Jason felt a tingle of fear. I wouldn't give someone off the street my number, he thought. Why would I give it to her?

"Uh, I gotta run."

"Oh, okay, Jason. Put me on your buddy list so you can see when I'm online."

"Sure, okay," Jason wrote, not sure what a buddy list was.

Jason logged off, wondering if it was common for people to ask for a phone number on the Internet. Oh, well, he thought, there's no way for Sue to find me, if Sue is actually her real name. Besides, there are plenty of Jasons on the Internet, and even more out in the real world.

Jason went to the kitchen for some juice, and before he'd even finished his glass, he felt the urge to log on again. Maybe this time he'd look for information on used cars . . . or other stuff.

He logged on and was greeted by a flashing banner promising that he'd find plenty of girls waiting for him in a chat room. Not knowing what a chat room was, Jason became curious. He clicked on the Connect icon and was quickly added to the list of chatters in a room called Town Square.

He stared at a white screen with colored script running up it. He read line after line of

"hello, Jason."

"welcome to our chat room, double-oh-seven."

"Hey, 007, howzit going?"

Jason realized that the whole room was talking to him.

"Hello," he typed.

Another box opened up on his screen. A box similar to the one Sue had used. "Hello, handsome," read the type. "I'm Monica. I'm 15, and I'm looking for some action. How's about you?"

Jason couldn't understand why a total stranger would be interested in action, or even what kind of *action* she was talking about. Was she offering sex? How would that work, he wondered.

Just then, Jason heard his mother's car pull up in the driveway.

His heart began to race. He made some kind of excuse and quickly logged out from the chat room. Then he ran up the stairs and slipped into bed. When his mother looked in on him, he pretended to be waking up and very, very drowsy.

"I tried calling you earlier, Jason," she said. "But the phone was busy."

"Yeah, Mom. It was the school asking where I was, so I told them I was sick."

"Well, that would have taken only a few minutes. Who else were you talking to?"

"Uh, a guy selling windows. I told him we weren't interested."

His mother seemed unconvinced, but she closed his bedroom door and headed down to the kitchen to make lunch.

Jason ate up in his room, waiting for his mom to leave for her afternoon appointments. She seemed to be hanging around the house forever, but she eventually left. As soon as she was gone, he was out of his bed and heading down to the basement.

In no time at all, he was logged on and back in the chat room.

"Hey, Jason. Welcome back."

Welcome back, thought Jason. Had people stayed in the chat room long enough to know that he had been there hours before? The thought of it scared him. How could anyone spend so much time on the Internet, let alone in just one chat room?

Within minutes of his arrival, he saw a new box open up. It was from someone named Ariana.

"Hey, cutie. I'm brunette, 5'4" and a pair of baby blues that'll make you smile. What's your name?"

This time, Jason remembered not to use his real name.

"I'm Dave."

"Hi, Davey."

Jason, as Davey, chatted with Ariana for quite some time, but in the end it was Ariana who had to log off.

"Kisses, Hun," were her last words as her dialogue box closed.

Jason went back into the chat room and hung around for a while until he read a line in bold black letters . . .

"type .p and whatever you write after that will be read only by me."

So Jason did just that.

And he wound up engaged in a long conversation with someone calling herself BABYDOLL. They talked about school, hobbies, shopping at the mall, and things they collected. Jason lied about almost everything, and he even made a few off-color remarks about gays and lesbians, just to show her how grown-up he was. What did he care? It was only the Internet, after all. No one knew who he was, and no one could ever call him on anything he said online.

It was just something he did for fun.

What harm could there be in that?

"Going to school today, Jase?"

"No, Mom, my throat feels worse. One more day at home, okay?"

Jason was well enough to go to school, but the possibility of flirting with BABYDOLL, CindyLou, and the others was enough of a reason for him to fake being sick just for one more day.

"Okay, but don't forget to have some chicken soup."

"Sure, Mom."

When Jason heard the front door close, he flew down the stairs like never before. And just moments after he had logged on, he was hit with four different chat boxes.

Each one had a cute opening line.

Jason ignored them all. He wanted to go back to the chat room and talk with BABYDOLL.

He scrolled down the long list of users inside the chat room, but he didn't see BABYDOLL anywhere. So Jason typed in: "Anyone see BABYDOLL?"

In response, he received a line in private, saying: "Hi, Jason007. It's me, BABYDOLL. Today I felt like being BABYCAKES."

Jason couldn't be sure who he was talking to, but he continued to chat with BABYCAKES anyway. After a while, it became obvious that BABYDOLL and BABYCAKES were one and the same person, since they both used the same words, tone, and writing style.

But just as Jason was getting more comfortable with BABY-CAKES, he received another message in private from someone named NightStalker. It read: "I know where you are. You can hide under the name 007, but I know who you are."

Jason was stunned.

"You're taking a long time to answer me, Jason," wrote BABYCAKES in the other box.

"Well," Jason wrote, "someone named NightStalker just told me in private that he knows where I live."

BABYCAKES responded: "Unless you give out your address or name, no one knows anything about you. Sounds like someone is just trying to scare you."

Well, if that was the plan, the guy was doing a good job of it. Jason *was* scared, really scared, especially since he couldn't be sure what – if anything – he'd done wrong.

"You think that's all it is?" Jason wanted to believe it.

"Probably. Now, where were we, babes?"

Jason tried to continue chatting, but he couldn't concentrate much on what BABYCAKES was saying, so he excused himself and logged out of the chat.

But he didn't quite log off from the Net. Instead, he went searching for information about chat rooms. He especially wanted to know if it was possible for someone to find out who you were and where you lived from a nickname. Jason's search turned up nothing, mostly because he wasn't sure what he was doing and where he should look. The search proved too frustrating, so he logged off, went upstairs, and crawled back into bed.

What if that person, this nut named NightStalker, really knew how and where to find him?

What if this person knew where he lived . . . and was outside his home right now? Jason was alone in the house, and maybe the NightStalker knew that too.

A chill ran the length of Jason's spine.

But when the shiver of fear had passed, he realized he was being silly. Ridiculous, in fact. Still, it wouldn't hurt to stay off the Internet for a few days, and never visit that chat room again.

Although Jason had missed a few days of school, he wasn't all that eager to return. Going to school meant he had to go outside, in public, where someone – someone named NightStalker – could be watching him.

It wasn't a good feeling.

But he managed to get through the day. On the way home, his friend Tom asked him, "Can I come over and see some of those adult sites you were talking about?"

"No," Jason answered quickly. "I promised my dad I'd rake leaves after school."

"How about tomorrow, then?"

"Yeah, maybe," Jason said, running up his driveway.

He opened the door with his key, slipped into the house, and locked the door behind him.

In the silence, he thought, What if this guy followed me to school, knew I wouldn't be home until now, and is hiding somewhere in the house? And now I've just locked myself in with this crazy man.

Jason didn't move. He felt his back press against the door with his hand still grasping the doorknob. He held his breath and looked around to see if everything looked normal.

Is this what the Internet can do to you?

He shook his head, tried to calm himself, and took a deep, deep breath. There *were* leaves to rake, but Jason wasn't about to go back outside. What if that guy drives by? Or worse, what if he stops . . . and confronts me. What will I do then?

He needed some advice, and the only one he could turn to, the only one who understood, was BABYCAKES, or Jessie, as she now wanted to be called. But whether she was BABYCAKES, BABYDOLL, or just plain Jessie, a whole week had gone by since he first met her, and that was too long.

Jason went downstairs, booted up the computer, and logged on.

He searched the chat rooms, but there was no BABYDOLL or BABYCAKES in sight. Maybe he'd send her an e-mail letting her know that he was on, and that he missed her and wanted to talk to her. That would be cool.

He clicked on the Send a Virtual Card button, but as he did this, a small white box appeared on his screen, sent to him by NightStalker.

"I know you're alone!"

Jason tried to ignore it.

"I know you go to Centennial High. I saw you there this morning."

Jason pulled back from the keyboard a moment. He aborted sending the card, then typed: "Stop it!"

No response.

"You can't scare me."

Nothing.

"You don't know how to find me, so go away."

"Oh, yes, I do know," came the response.

"How? Tell me how, you big phony."

"IP addresses."

Jason didn't know what IP addresses were.

"I'm going to the police," he wrote.

But when he sent the message, it came back saying that the other user had already logged off.

Jason's hands were trembling. He wanted to scream, tell somebody what was going on.

Jessie, he thought. He'd tell her all about it, ask her what he should do. Even the thought of her calmed him. He felt safe with her and enjoyed chatting with her. She liked him. She hung on every one of his words. She LOLed every one of his jokes.

But the more he thought about her, the more he realized that chatting with her on the Internet was no longer enough. He wanted to meet her, live and in person.

And then he wondered if it really was possible to find out who she was and where she lived through the IP addresses that guy had talked about.

Well, Jason had got better at conducting his Internet searches over the past few weeks, so while he waited for Jessie to log on, he searched the Net for info on IP addresses.

What he found made his blood run cold.

There it was on the screen, all the information anyone needed to know about how to locate and identify another person by his IP address. Jason didn't totally understand how it worked, but apparently every computer on the Internet emitted an identifier IP from which another user could get a name and address.

"Shit," Jason said out loud. His father was going to kill him . . . ground him for life. Take the damn computer away, maybe even the TV!

Jason felt his heart pounding in his throat when another white box opened up on his screen. It was from Jessie.

"Hey, where you been lately?"

"Busy with chores and stuff," Jason replied.

"All done now, huh? Wanna party?"

She was so understanding. So much fun.

"Actually, I was wondering if you'd like to meet."

"Sure! Where do you live?"

He typed in the city.

"What a coincidence – me too!"

Wow. Jason couldn't believe his luck.

"Do you know the City Center Mall?"

"I hang out there all the time."

"How about the food court, around 1 on Saturday?"

"I'll be there . . . the only blonde wearing a red leather mini and a Mickey Mouse patch on my jean jacket. HUGS X X X."

"I won't miss you, then."

"But I'll miss you . . . till then."

And she was gone.

The days seemed to take forever to pass.

Most of Jason's time was spent dreaming about Jessie dressed in a tight red miniskirt and a faded jean jacket with a Mickey Mouse patch on it. How cute was that? In comparison, he spent very little time worrying about the cyber-stalker who'd been hounding him. Apparently, Jason's mention of the police in their last exchange seemed to have got rid of the guy for good. Obviously he'd been trying to scare him, and Jason had to admit he'd done a good job of it. But at least Jason had learned his lesson from it, and now he knew to stay away from crazies on the Internet.

That stuff was all behind him now.

And in front of him – on Saturday, to be exact – was his meeting with Jessie.

They'd meet in the food court and talk for hours, and if they ended up becoming boyfriend and girlfriend, he'd never have to log onto the Internet again. They could chat on the phone, see each other at the mall, go see movies.

Who'd need the Internet any more?

When Saturday finally arrived, Jason tried not to watch the clock, but he couldn't help it. He was just too excited to do anything but count the minutes until he'd meet her.

The bus seemed to take forever to pick him up, and as he rode it, he read the overhead advertisements so many times he practically knew them by heart. Even the ad for condoms – which got him thinking.

He'd never even considered having a sexual relationship with Jessie – had thought only of holding her hand and planting a kiss on her cheek. Should he have considered buying condoms? The more he thought about it, the warmer he got in his clothes.

No. No sex.

We'll take things slowly at first, then see what happens.

The bus pulled up in front of the mall, and Jason got out. So many thoughts ran through his mind.

Was she going to be as cute as she said she was?

Was she going to be as sweet as Jason envisioned her?

Would she like the way he looked? Or would she think he was a loser?

When he entered the mall, he realized that he was forty minutes early, but that was okay. He could check out CDs in the music store and watch for her arrival from there.

And so he absently flipped CDs while looking out into the food court, his mind endlessly repeating the description she'd given him.

. . . the only blonde wearing a red leather mini and a Mickey Mouse patch on my jean jacket.

Jason hoped there hadn't been a sale on red leather minis the week before.

Just then, he noticed a young woman with a little boy sitting at one end of the bench next to the ice cream store. She had long blonde hair in tight curls, and yes, she wore a short red skirt. From a distance, Jason couldn't be sure if it was leather or not.

But it couldn't be her. She was with a little boy, most likely her son.

As the lady and the boy got up to leave, so did a girl on the other end of the bench. She got up and started walking toward the music store.

Jason watch her closely, but when she seemed to be looking his way, he looked down and pretended to be reading the liner notes of a CD.

She was getting closer. Close enough for Jason to see that she was wearing a skirt.

It was red, and it was short.

And it was made out of leather.

And she was blonde.

Now he just needed to spot the Mickey Mouse patch on her jacket. She was still too far away for him to have noticed such a detail, but as she came closer, he could make out the outline of a patch on the left side of her jacket.

The big ears and smiling face of Mickey Mouse were unmistakable.

She stopped next to the music store and looked at her watch.

Jason was about to put the CD down and ask if she was Jessie, but the blonde had stopped to adjust her hair, using the music store's window as a mirror.

Close up, Jason saw that her blonde hair looked like a wig that had been sliding down over her forehead.

He took another, better look at her. She wasn't that pretty for a fourteen-year-old. She also looked like she had a lot of makeup on. A lot.

This wasn't what Jason had envisioned.

She turned away from the store window and stared down the lane of shops . . . looking for him.

Then she moved to the bench next to the music store, but before she sat down, she looked around and proceeded to discreetly adjust her crotch.

Jason's mouth dropped open in horror.

Only a man would do something like that.

And then their eyes met . . .

Wasting Away

Sheri White

Stacy lifted the fork to her mouth and carefully drew the piece of steak inside, trying not to let her lips touch the stainless steel tines. She chewed the meat three times, careful not to swallow, then she spit the mangled piece of meat into her paper napkin as she wiped her lips. All the flavor – none of the calories. Stacy had the routine down to an art.

She ate some of the peas and a little bit of salad, but she politely declined the mashed potatoes and rolls her mother tried to foist on her, saying, "You eat like a bird, Stacy. You're nothing but skin and bones!" Luckily, her mother, exhausted as usual from working double shifts at the restaurant, would stare off into space while she ate and never noticed when Stacy spit out her food.

She would always take her own plate to the kitchen and scrape her meal into the garbage disposal. Then she would head up to her bathroom and weigh herself. If she was even half an ounce over ninety-five pounds, Stacy would either make herself vomit or pop a couple of the laxatives she kept taped to the back of the toilet.

She simply refused to get fat.

Tonight was a good night, though. The red LED readout on the bathroom scale showed a satisfying ninety-two pounds. Perhaps tomorrow morning, Stacy would splurge and have a piece of dry toast with her usual cup of black coffee.

She headed to her bedroom to perform the last part of her evening ritual. She stripped naked and stood in front of her full-length mirror. Not bad, she thought as she admired her skeletal figure. But you can look better than that. Skip the toast tomorrow morning. Obviously you've been eating too much. They'll have to wheel you to school on a dolly at this rate.

She wrapped herself in her robe and got busy with her homework.

The next morning, Stacy got up and did her exercises before showering. The morning ritual had begun. Next stop was the scale. Today she weighed ninety-three pounds. God, what a pig! No breakfast *or* lunch for me today! I'm such a whale. Disgusted with herself, she hopped in the shower, enjoying the hot spray of water on her always-cold body.

"Here you go, sweetie," said Stacy's mom as she entered the kitchen. "Cinnamon-apple pancakes, your favorite." She turned to smile at her daughter, but the smile faltered when she saw Stacy's appearance. Her jeans were practically slipping off her hips, and sharp ribs poked through her T-shirt. Stacy's hair, once thick and luxuriant, lay limply on her shoulders. Her skin was sallow, having lost its youthful, peachy sheen.

"No thanks, Mom. I need to get to school. I'll just grab a cup of coffee and drink it on the way."

"Stacy, please! Eat something before you go. You're so *thin*. You're wasting away to nothing right before my eyes." She sniffed back her tears, aware that her crying would only make her daughter angry.

Stacy rolled her eyes and chose a travel mug from the cupboard. "You're so dramatic, Mom." She poured the hot, black coffee into the cup and sipped it gratefully. "I'm not *that* thin. And I really need to be extra careful – I gained a pound overnight. A whole pound! I don't want to end up like that butterball Margie. She can barely bend over to tie her own shoes!"

Stacy's mom wanted to grab her daughter by the shoulders and shake some sense into her. Her little girl was trying to starve herself, and she had no idea how to stop it. Not even their family doctor had been able to help. He'd just told her that all the girls wanted to be thin these days and suggested she give Stacy a multi-vitamin.

Tears ran down her face as she watched Stacy go off to school.

ɤ

Stacy's lunchtime routine wasn't as difficult as breakfast and dinner. All of her friends were dieting – she was just best at it. She bought a bottle of water and a small salad before sitting down with her friends at their regular table.

"Have you seen Bruce lately? I think he's been working out – he looks so hunky!" Allison gestured to a blond boy in a Dallas Cowboys T-shirt across the room.

"I've had a crush on him for months," Stacy confided. "I'm hoping he'll ask me to the Winter Dance this year." Stacy blushed and took a small bite of lettuce. The group of fifteen-year-old girls dissolved into delighted giggles.

Except for one.

"He's cute and all, but there's no way I'd want to go out

with him," said Tammy. Stacy turned to her, wondering why the girl always had to be so negative.

"Why not? What's wrong with him?" Stacy took a sip of her water and waited for Tammy's answer, knowing that whatever it was, it would irritate her.

"Someone who looks like Bruce wouldn't want to date a girl who didn't look as hot as he does. Who needs that kind of pressure? I don't want to worry about every ounce of food that goes into my mouth." Tammy shrugged and took a bite of her veggie burger.

Stacy looked over at Bruce, who was talking and laughing with other football players. His arms were strong and muscular, his shoulders broad. Stacy knew that underneath his shirt, he probably had a washboard stomach. Not an ounce of fat on him. He'd never want to date an oinker like her.

Miserably, she pushed her salad aside.

❦

When Stacy got home from school, she noticed a plate of chocolate chip cookies on the kitchen table with a note that said "Love, Mom." She sighed angrily. Why doesn't she just give it a rest? How fat does she want to make me? Aren't I fat enough already?

She bypassed the cookies – They do smell good, though. If only they didn't have so many calories! – and opened the refrigerator for a bottle of water instead. As her hand touched the door handle, she gasped: she could clearly see the blue veins of her hand through the skin. Stacy slammed the refrigerator door and ran up to her room.

❦

Standing naked in front of the mirror, she was fascinated with what she saw. Her skin was translucent, not just on her hand but over her entire body. She could see the veins and arteries branching out from her heart and snaking their way through her body like tendrils. It was just like one of the pictures in her biology book, only this was flesh and blood. *Her* flesh and blood. Her mom would absolutely freak if she saw this.

Stacy got dressed, then masked her hands and face with beige makeup before heading back downstairs.

Dinner that night was a strained and quiet affair. Her mom glanced sadly at the plate of cookies still on the table. Stacy moved the food around her plate and occasionally chewed a piece of chicken before spitting it into her napkin. Suddenly, she noticed that her mother was watching this ritual with a horrified look on her face.

"Dear God, Stacy! Is *this* what you've been doing? Spitting out your food? No wonder you're wasting away to nothing! You've got to eat!"

"Oh, Mom, you're so dramatic! Chill out! That was just a fatty piece of chicken, that's all. It was gross, so I spit it out."

Stacy's mom slammed her hand on the table, making her daughter jump. "Don't you lie to me, young lady! Look at you – nothing but skin and bones! You're practically fading away in front of my eyes. I don't care what the doctor said. We're going to the hospital right now!"

She pushed back her chair, knocking it over. Ignoring it, she walked around the table and grabbed Stacy's wrist, but it slipped through her grasp, leaving smudges of makeup behind.

"What is this? Why are you wearing makeup on your hands?" She snatched a napkin off the table and wiped at Stacy's long, bony fingers, screaming at what she saw.

"Mom, please! Would you just relax? You're being ridiculous."

"We need to get you to the hospital right this instant, Stacy! You're sick . . . very, very sick!"

"I'm fine. Just leave me alone." Stacy got up and pushed past her mother, desperately wanting to get to her room. Her mother ran after her, but Stacy got to her room first and locked the door. She stripped off her clothes and looked in the mirror again. Now she could see most of her bones through her skin.

"Stacy, let me in! Let me help you!" Her mother rattled the knob and banged on the door.

"Go away! I'm fine!" Stacy preened in front of the mirror, liking what she saw. Maybe Bruce would ask her out after all. He'd be able to see for himself that her body was free of any disgusting fat.

Stacy turned at the sound of a key in the lock. Her mother burst into the room, her hands flying to her mouth in terror.

"Oh, my God! Stacy, you're . . . you're transparent! You look like a ghost." She ran to hug her daughter, but her arms went right through Stacy's body.

"Mom?" Stacy's voice trembled and a tear ran down her cheek. This was no longer cool – now it was just scary. "What's happening to me? I feel really funny!" She put her hands up in front of her face and watched in disbelief as they slowly disappeared.

Stacy's mom could do nothing but stand by helplessly and watch her only daughter fade away to nothing.

Playing the Game

Tanya Huff

He have his goodness now. God forbid I take it from him!" Mrs. Applegate closed the book and held it up against her chest. "All right, we've read the play. Would anyone like to explain what Arthur Miller was actually saying?" She peered around the class hopefully. "Anyone?"

Jennifer Katemon actually saw her wince as her rheumy blue gaze swept past. And returned.

"Jennifer?"

"Given that Miller wrote *The Crucible* in 1952, he was obviously creating an allegory for Senator McCarthy's" – she raised both hands to draw quotation marks in the air – "'witch hunts' against Communists in America and the hysteria surrounding them. A hysteria without substance that fed on itself. He wasn't even trying to be subtle."

Mrs. Applegate winced again, but Jennifer had stopped caring months ago. So what if most of the class wouldn't know an allegory if it bit them on the nose? She wasn't most of the class. She wasn't *any* of the class and saw no reason to hold herself back to their level.

"Does anyone else have an opinion?" the elderly English teacher asked without much hope.

"Yeah, I do."

Jennifer turned in surprise and received a challenging glare from under eyelashes so heavy with mascara they'd clumped into a solid mass. It wasn't news that Monica Jeffries had an opinion – the dyed black hair, the multiple piercings, the makeup, and the black thrift-shop clothes were a walking opinion as far as Jennifer was concerned. That Monica had an opinion that could actually be expressed – out loud and in class – now *that* was news. Even the school's other goths walked warily around her.

"I think," Monica continued as she slouched bonelessly back in her chair, "that the whole thing is a load. If those people had really sold their souls to Satan, then no way they'd have been hanged. They'd have called for him, and he'd have torn the town apart."

That started a discussion that went on until the end of the period.

Could we have wasted any more time? Jennifer wondered, gathering up her books and heading for her locker before the final bell stopped ringing. The group of jocks who hung around the football player two lockers down blocked her access, and she waited impatiently for them to move. Asking them to move was asking for trouble. Only two more months, she reminded herself as they left. Only two more months and you're . . .

"Didn't like not being the center of attention, did you, brainiac?" Monica leaned close enough for Jennifer to hear the soft clash of her silver bracelets and smell the faint scent of acrid smoke. "Didn't like that I had something to say, did you?"

"No, I didn't *care* that you had something to say."

Behind dark lipstick, the other girl's teeth came together with an audible snap. "You know," she purred, pivoting away on one chunky heel, "for someone so smart, you can be really stupid sometimes."

I was just thinking the same thing, Jennifer said to herself. She watched Monica walk to the end of the hall and join up with three silver-on-black friends. All four girls turned slowly toward her . . . and laughed.

When you are different, you have to keep a low profile. Have to. It isn't cool to be too smart. Well, it's okay to be smart, but it isn't cool to be aware of it. Trouble was, although she was very, very smart, Jennifer kept forgetting how the game was played. Take boyfriends. She wasn't bad-looking, and while she didn't pay much attention to clothes, her jeans and sweaters were pretty much the same as everyone else's. But she'd only ever gone out on one date. After the movie, parked out by the lake, he'd wanted to and she'd wanted to. She'd taken precautions just in case, and it had been fun. But apparently, it wasn't the way things were supposed to be done. She supposed that if she'd been stupid, she could have been the class slut, but straight-A students didn't go all the way. From all the muttering and the laughter, she gathered nobody went all the way – except her.

Once again, no idea of how the game was played.

Next year, pre-law. Then law school. Graduating top of her class. Great job. But first, surviving until the end of high school. Surviving Monica and her friends.

Closing her locker, Jennifer beat her head against the grimy metal.

It was going to be a *long* two months.

Monica wasn't in Jennifer's homeroom, but two of her friends were. As they went by Jennifer's desk the next morning, one of them pulled a wad of gum from between burgundy lips and ground it down into the top of her head. Glad she'd got her hair cut during March break, Jennifer reached up, grabbed the sticky mass, and snatched her fingers back from the sudden flare of heat.

Burning hot, bright pink bubblegum?

Not possible.

A second, more tentative grab revealed nothing more than a wet, rubbery clump that eventually pulled free. Same old, same old. So why did the giggling raise all the hair on the back of her neck?

The next day, the carton of milk she bought in the cafeteria was sour. The day after, her books flew off her desk in biology, waking Tad Baldwin from his regular after-lunch nap and directing the sarcastic side of Ms. Jones's tongue toward her for the first time that year.

"Y equals the co-efficient of the curve."

Mr. Ellis stared at her, heavy brows drawn in. "I didn't ask you, Jennifer."

"Yes, you did. I heard . . ."

Giggling. She heard giggling.

Then the pinching started.

Hard, twisting pinches when there was no one anywhere near her.

❦

"Hey, brainiac. How's it going?"

Unclenching her hands, Jennifer turned and managed not to flinch. Monica and all three friends were standing very close.

"Got plans this weekend? Some studying? A couple of extra-credit essays?" Monica asked, sneering.

"Stop it."

"Stop what? Showing an interest?"

"You know what."

"No." Leaning closer, breathing fumes of bitter herbs. "Tell me. Tell us."

"Stop . . . bothering me."

"No. We're still having fun. See you Monday."

The final pinch came just before all four girls turned the corner at the end of the hall.

Sighing, Jennifer laid her head against her locker door. I don't believe this is happening. I simply do *not* believe it. Unfortunately, it seemed her belief was unnecessary.

All things considered, the dead frog in her backpack was anti-climactic.

❦

"Look, Jennifer, I really, really need you to come over and help me out. Our final exam is in three weeks, and I don't have a clue what Mr. Ellis is talking about most of the time."

"You used to be good in math."

"Yeah, when math was about numbers, not letters. Please, Jen."

Roger Cilner was sort of a friend. Or had been sort of a

friend back before she'd left him in her intellectual dust. Channel surfing with the mute button on, Jennifer glanced up at the clock. Eight-twenty. Nothing on TV, and her parents wouldn't be home from their Friday night lecture series until ten.

"Look, I'm desperate here. I'll give you twenty bucks to tutor me."

She laughed. He sounded desperate, and after all, law school wasn't cheap. "I'll be right there."

Roger met her at the end of the street. "I didn't want you crossing the ravine alone. You know, it's dark and you're a . . ."

"Girl?" She'd actually planned to go around: cutting through the ravine wasn't smart. Still, a shortcut that was stupid for one person to attempt was a lot safer for two – even if Roger wasn't exactly her idea of a knight errant. Besides, it would cut twenty minutes off the walk. "Come on, then."

It was darker in the ravine than she remembered, although she hadn't been this way for some time. The light from the street lamps seemed to stop at the edge of the trees, and a crescent moon shed barely enough light to illuminate the path.

A sudden sound in the shadows sent Roger crashing to her.

Some Lancelot. "Don't worry, Roger, it's probably a squirrel."

"Wrong, brainiac. Not a squirrel."

A vicious pinch, and Jennifer took a deep breath of the pungent cloth shoved up against her face.

When she woke up, she was tied to a stake in a circle of black candles. Black candles? Oh, great. Ignoring the breeze that ruffled her hair, the flames burned straight and true.

Jennifer couldn't quite make out the pattern gouged into the ground, but all things considered, she didn't really need to see it to know what it was.

Thank you so much, Roger.

He'd obviously been a willing pawn, had probably traded her for immunity until the end of the school year. After what she'd been through over the past few days, she supposed she couldn't blame him.

Think, Jennifer, think. Use your head, don't lose it.

Being too smart had got her into this mess, and with any luck, it could get her out.

Just then, chanting from beyond the circle ghosted her bare arms with goosebumps.

Latin. They're chanting in Latin. They don't know Latin!

"Um, Monica? If you let me go now, I won't do anything about this. I mean, you've really got me, and you shouldn't . . . um, I mean . . ."

Not very articulate, but then this was her first time being tied to a stake in a dark ravine by four . . . um, witches? No, not witches. Witches practiced paganism, an earth-centric religion that had nothing to do with . . . Suddenly, her eyes widened, and if it hadn't been for the stake, her knees would have buckled. Latin held a number of words that were easy to translate. Words like *diabolus* and *sacrificium*.

"Do you guys even know what you're *doing*?"

Monica came forward into the candlelight, and Jennifer almost forgot how to breath. The dark-haired girl held a long, narrow knife in one hand, moonlight spilling down the blade.

Her heart pounding, Jennifer suddenly knew what the knife was for.

Sacrificium.

"Stop it!" She had to yell to be heard over the rising volume of the chanting. Probably no point in hoping the noise would attract someone passing by on the street, but she found herself hoping anyway. "You guys are playing with things you don't understand!"

Still chanting, Monica lifted her left hand to heart height and pushed the point of the blade into the fleshy base of her thumb. Then she tossed the knife into the circle.

It hit the ground at Jennifer's feet, a single drop of blood rolling off the tip.

Teeth clenched to hold back a moan, Jennifer closed her eyes.

The chanting stopped.

And the giggling started.

Giggling?

Jennifer opened her eyes to see Monica and all three of her friends draped over each other's shoulders and sharing a laugh at her expense.

"You should see the look on your face, brainiac. It's like you're not enjoying the ga –"

The earth inside the circle erupted, spewing out fire that took shape and acquired great arcing horns and an almost-clichéd tail but somehow never stopped being fire.

Then the screaming started.

Jennifer pulled free of the smoldering ropes and waited. When the dark figure returned, she bowed her head. Best not to look too closely at what it was chewing.

Monica and her friends had just been fooling around.

It seemed that, once again, she was the only one willing to go all the way.

Next year, pre-law. Then law school. Graduating top of her class. Great job.

No concerns about money.

And power. Lots and lots of power.

Guaranteed.

Easy to play the game when you write the rules.

The contract ended with a painful death at sixty-eight – but hey, sixty-eight was old – and then the usual payment.

Suddenly alone in the clearing, the fire gone, the ravine no more or less than it had been before, Jennifer sighed and stepped over the circle of melted candles. Two more months of high school made that eternity in hell seem almost inviting.

The Ghosts of Petroska Station

David Nickle

Slick frozen rain sheeted across the narrow windows of the classroom, like a flush down the back of a urinal. Todd gritted his swimming teeth and lowered his hand as Mr. Tokovich squinted across the sea of students at him. The old man licked his lips.

"Do you really have to go to the washroom? *Really*, Mr. Rung? Are you sure you aren't just getting a little bored with trigonometry, finding that my voice is droning a bit? Maybe you just want to go out and have a cigarette for a few minutes? Catch yourself a little nicotine *buzz*?"

Mr. Tokovich raised his sharp chin so he could look at Todd through the bottom half of his bifocals. He said "buzz" with a creepy kind of emphasis, like he had a mouthful of bugs to help him out with the "z" sound at the end. It was a cue for the rest of the class. They all turned to look at *Mr.* Todd Rung, the new kid whose dad had just transferred onto the base at Petroska a week ago. It made him crazy. Todd could have handled it if they were smiling or laughing at him – maybe even if a couple of the girls were whispering to each other and giggling. At least then he'd know where he stood.

But there was none of that at Petroska Station. They were all just staring, as if they were waiting for him to do something. Like maybe get out of there. Leave them to their own well-formed little cliques and clubs.

Todd wasn't going to let it faze him. "I don't smoke, sir," he said, keeping his eyes on Mr. Tokovich as he spoke. "I wouldn't know what a nicotine buzz is."

Mr. Tokovich's mouth twitched, as though it was thinking about smiling but knew the kind of trouble it would be in with the rest of Mr. Tokovich if it did.

"Then why," said Mr. Tokovich, "would you want to go to the washroom?"

Todd felt the glassy eyes of his classmates hot on him, like they were focusing the sun. It made him furious. Ever since his dad had got the transfer to army intelligence a year ago, he'd changed schools three times, not counting this one. He'd been in Germany and England and Greenland. And each time, it seemed like the first day dictated how the rest of his time there would go. First impressions counted, and this Mr. Tokovich was doing his level best to make sure the first impression Todd made here, at the base school in an Eastern European country whose name he couldn't even pronounce, was as geeky as could be. Todd set his jaw. There was no turning back.

"The same reason you do," said Todd, not looking away. "Sir. I've got to –"

"Enough!" said Mr. Tokovich again. His pale, sunken cheeks were flowering with a hint of pink. His eyes grew round. Mr. Tokovich did not like a wiseacre. "All right." He stepped around his desk, folding his hands in front of him. "You may go, Mr. Rung. Do you know where the washroom is in this old building?"

In fact, Todd didn't. It was only his first day in the school, and it was all he could do to find his way to this classroom on time.

"Because," said Mr. Tokovich around a fresh and malevolent smile, "some *children* find the twists and turns in Petroska Station a little . . . confusing. It was built by us Russians, after all, back when we were *bad* and hated little American boys like you. No shame in admitting you're out of your depth."

"I'm fine," said Todd. "Can I go?"

The class remained dead quiet. They stared at Todd like he was some strange specimen in biology class. Mr. Tokovich's smile broadened.

"Of course, my boy," he said. "At some point *everybody* has to go to the washroom."

Todd was sure he heard a collective intake of breath from his classmates as he hurried to the classroom's door.

Todd Rung closed the door behind him. He really did have to go to the washroom – and pretty badly. It was true that he didn't smoke, but when he turned fourteen, he'd started drinking coffee. At first, it was just one a day, with his dad over breakfast. But that had multiplied pretty quickly to three or four, depending. Coffee was not as bad as cigarettes, but it sure was habit-forming. And it did more to you than just keep you awake. Like now.

Todd hopped on one foot, then the other, as he looked up and down the long cinder-block hallway for any sign of a washroom. There was none. The hallway seemed to go about a hundred feet in each direction before it jogged. Nothing but blocks, some doors to other classrooms like the one he'd just come out of, and a few beat-up lockers that weren't even set into the walls.

One direction was as good as another, so Todd went right. It seemed to take forever to get to the corner. When he turned it, he groaned: the hall just went another fifty feet farther, then branched into a T. The teeth in the back of Todd's mouth were beginning to hurt. He clutched his belt buckle and went on to the T. Left or right? Both corridors went on for a while. The lights to the right were out after maybe thirty feet, though. "Left this time," he said. His voice echoed weirdly off the walls, as if he was yelling in the Grand Canyon or something. He didn't pay it any heed, though, and continued on. He came up to a pair of big double doors on his right. Full of hope, he pushed on them: at least they were different from the other doors. But they opened up on what looked like a gymnasium – a huge space as big as an airplane hangar, whose old hardwood floor was illuminated by spots from just two lamps dangling from an invisible ceiling. Todd made a noise of strangled frustration and let the doors swing shut. Where were the washrooms in this place?

He continued along as best he could. Todd felt his breath getting quicker as he turned corners, checked doors, and in one case doubled back to a narrow side corridor (which he'd caught out of the corner of his eye as he hurried past) and followed it to a door that opened into a long stairwell . . . which he climbed, even though it was dark.

For a moment, when he found the doors to the first two floors above him chained and padlocked, he was nearly overcome by a paralyzing terror. He probably would have screamed had not the padlock on the third-floor door been loose. The chains clattered on the concrete floor of the landing as he pulled open the door to find . . . another corridor. This one was barely lit at all – just a dim red light at the end, over another door like the one he'd come through.

He stood for a second, listening. Behind it, there was a sound like rushing water. Plumbing?

Maybe the flushing kind of plumbing?

The flushing kind of plumbing you'd find in a boys' room?

Todd suppressed a laugh. Finally!

He was about to start down the final corridor when he heard a noise behind him.

"That is not the answer, my friend."

Todd spun around and nearly wet himself right there. For an instant, he thought he was looking at a walking skeleton – it could have been a ghost roaming this huge, haunted old school. But the skeleton's lips pulled back in a smile.

Wait a minute, thought Todd. He's got lips. He wasn't anything but another kid. Another kid who was really skinny, cut his hair really short, and from the looks of his skin hadn't seen daylight in a really, really long time.

And he spoke with a funny accent. Todd thought it might be Russian.

Todd looked back at the red light.

"Unwise," said the boy.

"Look," said Todd, "I've *really* got to go."

"That," said the boy, "is not the privy. That is merely what they want you to believe."

"Privy?" He hadn't heard it called a privy in years. "Okay. That's not it. Show me where one is."

"Ah." The boy nodded, more to himself than to Todd. He stepped back into the stairwell and pointed down.

Todd's good sense told him not to go there. He should just break off from this kid, run down to the end of the hall, to the door where the red light shone, and do his business.

But there was something in the boy's hollowed-out eyes: a pleading, a knowing, and most convincingly, an underlying terror at what lay behind that door with the pulsating light over it.

"Hurry," said the kid. "They almost have you."

Todd swallowed and, gripping his belt buckle so hard it hurt, stepped back into the stairwell. The boy shut the door. Before it finished swinging, Todd swore he saw the door at the other end of the corridor start to open.

"The first thing," said the boy as they climbed down the stairs, "is to know this: that was no privy. It was a trap for you. There are no privies here."

"What? What kind of a school doesn't have a . . . a washroom?"

The boy smiled wryly. "Good question," he said. "The answer is simple: no kind of school. This is not truly a school."

Todd squinted at the boy. "Then – what? – should I just go to the washroom now?"

The boy shook his head. "No," he said. "If you do that, they'll find you."

"Find me?"

"You would not even be allowed to finish."

Todd stopped and leaned against the railing. It was better when he stood still. His bladder still felt like it was a water balloon, but the walking was making it worse. He looked at the boy.

"Who are you?"

"You may call me Gregor."

"Greg."

"Greg-*or*," he said. "You are not in New York City any more."

"Obviously," said Todd. He crossed his arms and stared at Gregor in the dim stairwell. Just what was a kid like this doing here? The school was on an *American* military base. It was *supposed* to be New York City – supposed to be just like home for the families that were stationed here.

But this place . . . This place was nothing like home.

And this kid Gregor – he didn't belong here. Any more, thought Todd, than he did himself.

"How did you get . . . here?"

"In the halls?" Gregor appeared to consider this. "Much like you did. I was brought here some time ago by my parents. I enrolled in a class. I watched as my classmates became . . ."

"Weird?" Todd thought about those stares he'd been getting.

"Distant," said Gregor. "A better word. Not themselves."

"I have noticed that too," said Todd. "Why're they like that?"

"Because," said Gregor, "they have been here longer than you. They are among the first wave of Americans to come to our base. They have already been brainwashed."

"Brainwashed?"

Gregor nodded. "That is what this place is for. Like in old spy movies, yes? They are very good at it here. Now come on. We have to keep moving."

Gregor grabbed his arm to pull him along. But Todd stood his ground. "No," he said. "*Brainwashing*. You're messing with me. You have to tell me what's going on here."

"What's going on here" – Gregor gave a sharp tug at Todd's arm – "is that if you stay still, you will lose yourself."

"Lose myself." Todd took a breath and gritted his teeth. He gave Gregor a sideways glance. "Right. I'm thinking I'm going to lose something if I don't find a washroom soon."

Down and down and farther down. It didn't take long for Todd to lose track of how deep they'd gone. Five floors? Eight? Ten or more? The walls were slick and sweaty, and somewhere a pipe dripped steadily into an unseen pool of water. Todd could barely see straight because he had to go so badly.

Finally, they came to the bottom. Todd looked longingly at the open drain in the concrete floor, but Gregor slapped him on the arm.

"No! What did I tell you?"

Gregor led Todd across a flat concrete floor between tall metal posts and walls of steel mesh. They came to a door that had a special lock on it with a keypad like a calculator. Gregor punched the keys, and somewhere in the wall, Todd heard the rasping sound of metal teeth moving through gears. Then there was a single click and the door swung open. The stairwell was flooded with silvery light.

"This is the safe place," said Gregor. "They have never found us here. We are able to survive and keep a measure of ourselves."

"A measure of ourselves. Right." Todd blinked in the light. "Who are *they*?"

Gregor led him through the door. Todd heard it swing shut behind them, finally closing with a noise like the clang of a bank vault.

"All the students," said Gregor. "The station command. Your teacher is probably one of them. So are the rest."

Todd's eyes adjusted quickly to the brightness. They were in a large room filled with tall machinery. The floor was concrete. Light came from a bank of fluorescent lamps hanging on chains from the very high ceiling.

There were others here. Others like Gregor – thin and ragged, like human skeletons. They stared at Todd. And they were smiling.

"Now," said Gregor, his own smile broadening to make his face look more like a skull than ever, "you are one of us. A ghost of Petroska Station." Gregor raised his voice to speak to the others. "Let us welcome our new ghost!"

The assembly of the dead stepped closer to Todd. He got a better look at them. There were boys and girls there – some younger than him, but most a couple of years older. Their faces were all thin and drawn. Red rimmed their eyes, and their lips were pulled tight across their teeth, which seemed very sharp.

Todd flinched. He'd never had to pee so badly in his life, and the terror that was coursing through him didn't make it any easier to hold it in. What had he got himself into? Some weird cult in the basement of the station school? Something even worse?

He'd rather be among those weird kids up in trigonometry than down here. He'd gone to the washroom and stumbled straight into some weird Eastern bloc kid cult hell!

"Get away from me!" Todd tried to open the door, but it had a keypad on this side as well, underneath a fire extinguisher that looked about a hundred years old. Without the access code, Todd was as good as staring at a blank wall.

Todd turned back to the ghosts. "Get back!"

They stopped advancing on him but didn't back off.

"My friend," said Gregor. "Please keep calm. You're safe here. We're all safe here."

Todd looked at the long, thin faces before him. He didn't feel safe at all. These weren't kids – they were monsters. Like they said: ghosts.

They started toward him again.

"I said get back!"

Before Todd knew what he was doing, he'd reached back, grabbed at the big wheel on top of the fire extinguisher, and pulled it down. It weighed a ton, but he hefted it in front of him. There was a pin – like a hand-grenade pin – blocking the wide trigger. He yanked it out, and before they could get any closer, he opened up. The room seemed to fill with white foam.

"You idiot!" shouted Gregor. "What are you doing?"

Even if he'd had time to think about it, Todd knew he wouldn't be able to answer that question properly. He felt adrift from everything right now. He'd started the day in a new school, surrounded by new kids in a class that had been going on for months before he'd shown up. That was nothing he hadn't done before. Eventually, he would have adapted to this place the same way he'd adapted to Germany and England. Brainwashing. This place was the brainwashing.

But once he'd stepped into this hall, all bets were off. It was worse than the Dungeons and Dragons crowd in Greenland. There at least they'd only played at being lost in a maze of monsters. But here . . .

Two monsters stepped out of the fog of fire-retardant. One was like Gregor – thin as a skeleton, with just a few patches of cemetery white hair on its knobby scalp. Another was shorter, thicker about the chest, with eye sockets deep enough to reach to the back of its skull.

At the sight of them, Todd felt his breath catch in his throat and a warm spot dampen his shorts. And at that moment, an even more primal horror came over him.

He was peeing himself.

Todd hadn't done that since . . . since he could remember.

"No way," Todd said through gritted teeth. He screwed his eyes shut and summoned every inch of willpower he had. "No . . . way."

It was as if Todd was trying to stop the flow of a river after it had burst over a formidable breakwall. But he held his breath and balled his fists, and soon the warm spot in his shorts had stopped growing. He let out his breath in a long, ragged stream.

When he opened his eyes, he found himself looking into Gregor's. Todd swore. He'd stopped the peeing all right, but he'd been working at that so hard that he'd let the two monsters – the two ghosts of Petroska – lay hold of him at the shoulders.

Gregor smiled.

"Good," he said, stepping back into the little blizzard of airborne fire-retardant. He turned to the others and shouted something in Russian. Todd saw them nod, then he felt a jolt as his two captors started to drag him along after Gregor and the rest of them.

ɞ

Down and along and deeper still they went. Todd was barely able to think now – his jeans were cold and damp against his thighs, and he'd never felt more miserable. He made the barest note of the subterranean world that went by him: tall metal things like old computers filled a hall that they crossed; at one point, it seemed as though they crossed over a chasm on a narrow metal bridge held up by black chains; next, they squeezed through a corridor dark and narrow; then they went down more stairs until the walls were bare rock.

Finally, they came to a metal-sheathed door set straight into the rock.

"Inside," said Gregor as a thing that might have once been a girl pulled up a crossbar and swung the door open.

Someone gave Todd a push, and he stumbled in.

The door swung shut. He was alone and in the dark beyond the door.

"Hey!" He pressed himself up against the metal of the door. He couldn't hear a sound through it, and no one could probably hear him either. But that didn't stop him from yelling. "Hey! What have you done? Where am I?"

Todd let himself slide down the door. He might as well die here, completely alone. Abandoned even by the ghosts.

This room had a smell to it, though. It smelled sharp and musty – like a washroom. A washroom where the plumbing hadn't been fixed since the Cold War.

As his eyes adjusted to the darkness, he saw it was worse than that. The walls of the room were bare concrete. The floor was bare rock, and it sloped down to a hole in the middle of the room – a hole maybe a foot and a half around. As he listened, a gurgling sound came up.

Todd looked at it in horror. He was supposed to go *there*? It was hideous. He would rather have found a corner in the hallway.

He buried his face in his hands.

"Humph, Mr. Rung." A sniffing sound. "It is true."

Todd's hands dropped away. The voice was coming from nearby. Maybe as near as his ear.

He turned around.

Mr. Tokovich was standing behind him.

"Everybody," continued Mr. Tokovich, "has to go to the washroom sooner or later."

"Mr. Tokovich? What are you doing here?"

"And you," said the voice that sounded like Mr. Tokovich's, "had your accident a little sooner than later, yes?"

Todd felt blood rush to his face. The spot in his pants was awful and clammy. Thanks for reminding me, he thought.

"But," said Mr. Tokovich, "it was only a little accident. You stopped yourself, didn't you?"

Todd nodded. "It wasn't easy," he said.

"No, it isn't easy. It goes against every animal instinct to hold something like that inside. It probably goes against our better interests, if you stop and think about it."

Todd felt a hand on his shoulder now. The fingers felt very long – their tips seemed to dig into his ribs.

"But of course, after a while you stop thinking. Because the fact that you did manage to defeat your urge suggests that you've got another instinct in you – one more developed. Stand up, Mr. Rung."

As the voice spoke, the fingers seemed to lift Todd to his feet. He felt like he was swimming as he stepped away from the door.

"Good boy. Now, do you still have to relieve yourself?"

Todd nodded. Tears streamed down his face.

"Then why don't you? Right here? In that wonderful *pit* there? That, after all, is why those horrible creatures brought you to this place."

"Wh-what?"

The voice laughed. "Don't you know what this is?" it said. "You are in a lavatory. A privy. A toilet. The *washroom*. If you go here, you're released! That's what they say down here! You may join – if you wish – the ghosts, those horrible lonely little children, and leave the world of" – and here the word hissed – "civility."

"They . . . they told me you were brainwashing kids," said Todd.

Mr. Tokovich smiled. "My my," he said. "Brainwashing. What a word. So dramatic. *Brainwashing*! With the flashing lights and the needles full of funny serums." He laughed now. Todd laughed too. It *was* pretty funny the way Mr. Tokovich put it.

"You don't have to brainwash somebody to make him your friend," said Mr. Tokovich. "You just have to offer him a choice. Show him the alternatives. And you have a very clear choice. Here is your washroom, Mr. Rung. Do you wish to use it?"

"No," said Todd. He had a sudden picture of himself, skinny as a skeleton, his hair just a thin velvet over a bone white scalp, wandering the dark halls underneath Petroska.

"Good. You have chosen civility over your animal nature." Tokovich paused. "You can hold it awhile longer?"

Todd swallowed. "Yes."

"Excellent."

With that, there came a loud clanking sound and the door swung open. The light on the other side was blinding. Stepping into it would be like crossing a threshold.

"Go on," said Tokovich. "Make up your mind."

"One question," said Todd.

"Ask anything."

"What's going to happen to Gregor and . . . and the ghosts now that you've found their hideout?"

Tokovich smiled. "Nothing," he said, "ever happens to the ghosts. They have already made their choice. And they serve their purpose – helping you to make yours."

Before he could think about that any further, Todd lifted his foot and stepped into the light.

ঀ

The sky outside the narrow windows of the math class was clear and bright; if you looked, you could even see the distant mountain peaks caught in sunlight that made their snowy tops into something like hammered gold. No one looked at them now, though. Everyone's eyes were darting between Mr. Tokovich and the new kid, Todd Rung.

"Yes, Mr. Rung?"

"May I please be excused, sir?" Todd spoke with great care. It was his first day back in regular classes after taking a couple of days off to go over things with Mr. Tokovich and the station command. Todd thought it was like a second chance – another first day at school, just like the last one. But this time, he wasn't worried that he wouldn't fit in, that he wouldn't have friends here. The one thing he'd learned was that everyone was his friend at Petroska Station. It was obvious to Todd, even if it wasn't obvious to his father, who'd just looked away and set his lips angrily when his son had tried to explain it to him last night. Todd thought he might have seen a tear forming at the corner of his father's eye. The older man finally just said he was sorry over and over again – so sorry for bringing Todd here, sorry for wanting to go into intelligence work so badly he'd forgotten about his only son.

"You have to go to the washroom again?" said Mr. Tokovich now. He regarded Todd through the bottom of his bifocals, then he smiled in a warm and friendly way. "Very well. You're a level boy – a *trustworthy* boy. You know the way."

"Yes, sir. Thank you, sir."

Todd stepped out into the hallway. He didn't see what his father had to be upset about. After all, having gone from place to place, country to country, Todd had finally found a way to fit in. And not with those Dungeons and Dragons geeks either – not on the fringe. It made Todd want to smile all the time.

Well, it made *most* of Todd want to smile. He was faintly aware of a small part of himself that didn't smile much since he'd returned to class. Maybe, thought Todd, it was that part of him, that ghost of the boy he had been, that had asked to go to the washroom now.

Because Todd found he didn't really have to go to the washroom much since he'd stopped drinking coffee. He sure didn't have to go now, as he stepped around a corner into one of the many, many dark spaces in old Petroska Station and struck a wooden match against the brick there.

"G-Gregor?" he said, peering into the dark by the flame of the flickering match. "Help me – please."

But Gregor didn't answer. And why should he? Todd had made his choice, after all. He'd chosen civility, and that pretty much ruled out Gregor and the ghosts of Petroska Station.

It wasn't long before the match flame flickered and the hall went dark again. And it wasn't long after that that Todd was able to pull himself together and go back to class.

To the Lonely Sea and Sky

Tom Piccirilli

Summer had come to an end, and the dark weather of autumn began to roll in across the waters.

We still didn't have our driver's licenses, but Boone could captain his seventeen-foot Silverline boat to Echo Island much faster than most folks could drive over the causeway. We'd chip in for gas and fill the cooler with thick roast beef sandwiches from Dougie's Deli. All summer long, we fished and water-skied, and when the cool winds came down from the north and the beaches emptied, we took slow rides out to the point to drift in the shadow of the lighthouse.

Eight of us grew up and ran around together, but the economy of the south shore had got so bad over the past few years that families were migrating in droves. Now only three of us were left: Boone, Jules, and me. They called me Doc because once I'd set a bird's broken wing before getting it to the vet. Sometimes you pick up a nickname for the dumbest reasons, and it sticks with you forever. We were all sixteen and just waiting until we could get out into the world with everybody else. Sometimes it felt like we never would.

Boone had put on a lot of muscle in the past year or so. He stood nearly six feet tall and had a bushy halo of golden red hair and the pointed chin fuzz of a goatee. He was tan and lean and a little lost. His mother had run off with a shoe salesman more than a year ago, and Boone and his dad had both become a lot edgier, filled with an anger that could cut loose at any second.

Jules was so pretty that it almost hurt to look at her. She had short black hair that framed her heart-shaped face, and her nutmeg eyes were filled with a kind of wild light that sent shivers through me. She had a sweet giggle that made me ache inside. It was a strange feeling, considering she was my best friend.

Once I'd been able to talk to her about anything at all, but lately it had become difficult for me to speak to her about even normal stuff. I didn't know exactly when I'd fallen in love with her, but now that I had, it felt as if I'd been this way forever.

This day, we sat on Boone's boat, swaying to the light waves in the channel, tied to the dock. Jules turned her face to the sky and bathed in the dying heat, arms outstretched and hands open as if she was trying to catch broken promises or rose petals.

We all wore shorts, but Jules and I had also put on sweat-shirts. The day was overcast and the breeze had a chill to it. Boone refused to believe that summer was over and wouldn't even wear a pullover. The goosebumps stood out on his bare chest and back, and he occasionally shivered, yet he wouldn't give in.

It was Sunday and I had to get home to finish up my algebra homework, but I didn't want to leave the two of them together. As much as I cared about Jules, I knew that she felt the exact same way about Boone. She tried to keep him out of trouble but hadn't been able to do much for him lately. His grades were slipping, and he kept getting into fights all the time.

He laid back in his seat with his shades on, as if the sun was burning down on him. Jules said, "Boone, did you finish your paper on Poe for English?"

"No."

"It's due tomorrow."

"I know. I'll get to it tonight."

"You won't have time to read the story assignments."

He took a deep breath but didn't sit up. "It's all online anyway. A little cut and paste, and the report will be fine."

Jules frowned, but he didn't see it. "You're already riding a D in the class."

"Plenty of time to make up for those stupid quizzes."

"But –"

This kind of discussion went nowhere fast on a Sunday afternoon, especially with Boone, so I interrupted. "I've got a ton of algebra to finish up. How about a quick ride out to the bridge and then back? It'll be pretty late by then, and we can all get started on our homework."

Jules said, "Sounds okay to me."

Boone snatched off his sunglasses and stared up at the dull gray sky as if Jules and I had darkened it ourselves. "Geez, don't you people ever talk about anything but school? This is probably our last weekend out here, you know. My dad's going to want to dry-dock the boat soon."

He opened the cooler, grabbed a can of beer, and drank almost all of it in one long pull. During the summer, he and I had shared our first six-pack together, taking it from his father's box fridge in his small workshop. I'd hated the taste of it and how it made me feel – all wobbly and out of control. We'd tried a little of his dad's whiskey too, and we'd both wound up drunk and sick. I couldn't even go near the stuff any more because the smell took my knees out, but Boone had acquired a taste for it. He'd got himself a little flask and occasionally took nips out of it when we went over to Echo Island.

"I've got an idea too," he said. "But you're not going to like it, Doc."

"Then let me just say no now and get it out of the way."

"At least hear me out."

Jules folded her hands inside her sweatshirt and asked, "What is it, Boone?"

He gave a sidelong glance and a grin that made my stomach sink. "Let's go to the lighthouse and find ourselves a ghost."

Any other time and it might've sounded like fun, but the chill had deepened and the wind came off the water, encircling us like invisible arms. The marina was empty, and it seemed as if we were the only people on earth right then. Jules smiled, but there was sorrow in it. I wanted to do nothing more than get her off the boat and walk her back home. The nape of my neck tingled and grew itchy, and I scanned the jetty because it felt like somebody was watching me.

The lighthouse had long been rumored to be haunted. People talked of dead faces in the tower and eerie, unearthly sounds that filled the night. My own father claimed to have seen something there years ago. He never told me what, and despite my curiosity, I never asked.

Jules said, "I think we ought to just take a ride out to the bridge and then get to work on your paper. I'll help you, if you want."

"No," he said, and his voice had a deep thrum to it that bordered on rage. "I thought you guys were my friends."

"We are."

"Then quit acting like a couple of vice-principals and let's just go have some fun." That subtle anger that always lurked just under his surface was starting to come to the top. Boone could become irate over nothing much, and Jules and I didn't want to see that.

"Okay, let's go to the point," I said.

"Aww, you guys are the best!"

"Of course we are," Jules told him.

He nabbed another beer. Our eyes met, and he almost dared me to say something. I touched his shoulder and said, "Don't, Boone."

"Don't what?"

"Don't have another drink."

"Why not?"

"We just decided that you're taking us over to the point."

"So?"

"So I don't want you handling your boat when you've had too much."

He was still grinning, but his lips seemed painted onto his face. "Hey, you telling me what to do?"

"In this case, yeah."

"You can either come or stay, I don't much care any more. But I do what I like, and you don't run the show."

Jules remained quiet. I knew she would follow him no matter where he led. Since I was in love with her, I had to go along.

I had to think of her.

We packed up the Silverline, and Boone had some trouble getting us out of dock. He handled the lines poorly, and instead of letting us drift in reverse until we were in the channel, he gunned it and nearly rapped into a guide pole.

It took twenty minutes to get out to Turtle Hill Point, and we didn't talk much the entire ride. I watched Boone carefully – he seemed to be enjoying himself, the sea spray in his face. The wind rose, but he still wouldn't put a shirt on.

Jules and I sat in the corner seats. Occasionally we hit some rougher waters, and Boone would let out a yee-haw as the boat lifted and slapped back down again. I kept wondering where his flask was and if he'd had any of his father's whiskey today.

"You okay?" I asked her.

"Sure," she said.

"A little late in the day to go ghost hunting, isn't it?"

"We'd have better luck spotting them at night, I suppose. But if this is our last weekend of the season out here, then let's make the most of it. We can humor him a little."

Black clouds wafted in the pale sky as the roiling waves lapped along the beaches. Finally, we rounded the edge of the shoreline and came into view of Toad Hill.

A light mist cloaked the lighthouse, and sea gulls soared just above the surf. The sandstone blocks at the base of the building proper looked as if they'd sprung from the rocky soil of the plateau itself. The tower rose to 107 feet, and I knew that inside there were ten stories of iron steps spiraling to the top.

The lighthouse had been completely automated twenty-five years ago. My father still told tales of when he was in the coast guard and vessels were dependent on the lightkeepers to lead them safely toward the bay.

The lighthouse had been erected at the extreme west end of the Toad Hill plateau, a hundred yards off from the bluff. The point had been eroded over the past century, and now the tower stood less than fifty feet from the edge of the bluff face. Boulders formed a seawall to try to break the force of the storms, but every year, waves and rain caused more soil to fall into the ocean.

Boone was coming in too fast. I reached for the wheel and said, "You're going to ground us."

"Take your hands off."

"Listen –"

"Sit back down, Doc."

I seized the shift stick and threw it into neutral, shut off the motor, and yanked out the key. We floated in, and the bottom scraped lightly against rocks. If we hadn't stopped when we did, the propeller would've chewed into stone and blown the engine.

Boone said nothing and neither did Jules. I tossed the anchor over and threw the bumper cushions over the sides to keep the boat from being scratched.

"All right, so where are the ghouls and critters?" he asked.

My father *had* told me that he'd seen something through his binoculars from about four nautical miles out. He and his crew had been returning to Echo Island from a search-and-rescue mission. A trawler had lost power in a storm, and they were towing her back to safe waters.

"The dead don't rest on Toad Hill," he'd said, and I believed him.

At last, Boone decided to put on a pullover sweatshirt. He took a half-finished beer with him and hopped off the starboard bow, stepping across the pools and eddies until he was up on the rocks of the butte. Jules followed him, carefully winding her way across the seawall until they made it to shore.

I felt hesitant. A part of me didn't want to go at all. I stared up at the gleaming windows of the lighthouse, expecting tragic and hollowed spectral faces to be looking down at me. There were none.

The wind had grown stronger, and the late-afternoon sky became even more dark and overcast.

"Are you coming or not?" he asked, taking one last sip of his beer. He threw the can into the water. Jules looked at me and gave a small, sad smile that made my chest go soft and warm.

"Yeah," I said, "I'm coming."

The building proper had been taken over by a historical society and turned into a small museum. There were drawings and maps and photos of slave ships, whaling vessels, and the island as it had looked a century ago. In the next room was a little gift shop that sold foam mug holders, keychains, calendars, and postcards.

A girl of about twenty worked the counter, and only one other staff member – a guy around that same age – was in sight. He kept leaning over the cash register and whispering to her, and she smiled shyly and mumbled back. They paid no attention to us.

We walked around the museum and looked at all the old-fashioned pictures and documents. Boone stared at a portrait of a whaling captain and said, "You expect he's still here? Old Captain – what's his name? – McDonnell. Says he was lost at sea. Think he found his way back here?"

Jules considered it seriously. "No, I don't believe so."

"Why?"

"It says he was survived by a wife, four children, and nine grandchildren. They all lived right out on the island, over in Amaghansett. Anybody with a large family like that wouldn't wander an old lighthouse."

"He commanded a vessel," Boone said, "and went down with the ship. A sailor's life is the sea. That's all he really loves."

"Maybe for some of them," Jules said, staring at the

captain's face. "But he has friendly eyes, like my grandfather. I bet he cherished coming home to his wife and kids."

"I agree," I said. "Only sailors without families would ever stick around this place."

"You mean like me?" he said.

I could tell he wanted to say a lot more about his mother, but he held it in. I wondered how much longer he could go on like that, never saying what he needed to say.

"Hey, you kids," the staff member called, "if you go up the tower, don't stray over the yellow line at the top. Don't climb the last set of five stairs."

"Okay," I said.

"I mean it."

"It's all right. We won't."

We turned to the ancient wood door with the iron brackets and small stained-glass window that led to the tower. Boone grabbed the heavy handle and started up the steps. Jules and I followed.

So we climbed.

The stairway spiraling up the tower was dank, dark, incredibly steep, and difficult to maneuver. The walls were chipped, and the brickwork had been eaten at over the years by the salt air. I hadn't visited the inside of the lighthouse since our class trip back in fourth grade. At the time, I'd thought it a grand and magnificent place. Now I realized it was just ugly and depressing.

There was no headroom at all, and Boone had to duck as he led us. If another tour had been coming down as we went up, we'd all be stuck. The only space came when we reached one of the immense window frames. Each one had a large concrete sill. There were caution signs everywhere. Do Not Sit. Do Not Attempt to Open Window, Alarm Will Sound. Watch Low Ceiling.

By the time we got halfway to the top, Jules and I were wheezing and gasping.

"I didn't know I was this out of shape," she said.

"I knew I was," I told her, "but I didn't want to believe it."

"My knees are killing me."

"Mine too."

"But at least my thighs are getting a workout."

"They don't need it."

That made her giggle again, and the sound floated up and down the tight stairwell.

Boone kept sipping whiskey. He tried to hide it from me because he was farther ahead in the shadows, but the stink of his breath gave him away. When we got to the next huge window frame, I saw that his eyes had a glaze to them. He'd had too much to drink and his smile had loosened up, so he leered like an idiot. He couldn't help himself.

Jules reached down to me and grasped my shoulder. "Come on, Doc, just a little farther to go."

"This thing is higher than Mount Everest."

"Sure feels like it."

"How'd we climb this in fourth grade?"

"I think we had wings on our ankles back then."

Finally, I saw the catwalk at the top of the tower coming into view, all those railings and panes of glass surrounding the massive lens and giant light bulb itself. I felt a drop of rain splash against my forehead.

The yellow line was clearly marked at the fifth step from the top. I could remember our fourth-grade teacher yelling at each of us in turn not to cross the line. Boone stepped right up the last couple of stairs and disappeared onto the walkway.

"Boone, knock it off," I called. "Just take a look around."

"It's fine," he said from out of sight. "There are plenty of rails here, and that guy downstairs isn't about to give us any trouble."

"I don't think we should," Jules said.

"Oh, come on!"

Boone reached back down and took Jules's hand. He grinned at her, and after a moment's hesitation, she allowed him to draw her over the yellow line and up to the very tip of the lighthouse.

"Oh, look how beautiful."

I moved up to the top step and held on to one of the railings. A hundred feet below, the waves crashed into the seawall. The sky had grown black, and in the distance, storm clouds flashed lightning. The wind brushed harshly against us, rattling all that glass.

"Doc, isn't it gorgeous out here?"

"Yes, it is," I admitted.

Boone was moving much too quickly across the walkway, sort of racing around the tower and looking at every view. "All right, so where are the ghosts?"

"It's cold out here," I said. "Maybe they went in to warm up near the fireplace."

"Old Captain McDonnell's spirit might've gone home to his family, but there must be a few lonely phantoms wandering around." He looked over the side and let out a mocking screech.

I stepped closer. The smell of the whiskey and beer on his breath made my stomach turn. "You've had enough," I said into his ear.

"What?"

"Quit drinking now. Come on, let's go. If we leave now, we might miss the storm."

He turned on me with such a gaze of loathing that I was nearly forced back. "You're really starting to get on my nerves, Doc. You're beginning to sound like my old man."

To Boone, that was the worst insult he could give, comparing somebody to his father. The two of them had always had a troubled relationship, but when his mother left, things had got much worse.

It was becoming slippery up on the metal catwalk. Jules slid and let out a squeal, and I caught her in my arms. The rain came down much harder, slapping the immense light with such force that it slowly spun on its well-oiled gears.

"I'm going now," I said.

"Doc, wait," Jules called, but I was already walking toward the stairs. I looked back over at them, pleading to Jules with my eyes. She smiled sadly at me.

Boone sneaked another drink, but the flask slipped from his fingers and dropped to the deck. He stooped to pick it up, and his feet skidded out from under him. He tried to keep his balance, waving his arms wildly, but it was no good.

He landed wrong and let out a little "Whuff," and with a strange whirling motion, almost as if he'd planned it all out, he rolled in the puddling rain and fell over the side of the catwalk.

I screamed his name and Jules spun. Boone clung to the bottom railing, laughing ashamedly but with eyes filled with fear. He flailed, and his wet hair hung in his eyes. Jules cried out. Boone's lips curled and turned white. He'd sobered up quickly and tried to keep from shrieking. So did I.

He yelled, "Hey, guys, I could use a little help here!"

"Boone, hold on!"

"What else did you think I'd do?"

"Don't let go!"

"Thanks for the advice, Doc!"

I scrambled toward him, but there was no room to move on the catwalk. Jules ran forward, just a couple of feet in front of me, and I watched as Boone's fingers started to slip from the railing. She reached out in a graceful arc and almost managed to grab his wrist. She clawed for him, missed, and tumbled past the rail.

I shrieked and dove with both my arms outstretched. Boone gripped my left hand and struggled to climb up. He got a hold of my shoulder and drew himself back up to the walkway, gasping.

But where Jules had been there was only the wind and the rain and the sound of the surf thrashing below.

She was gone.

Wailing, Boone fell to his knees, and he kept crying her name until the two staff members came rushing up and helped me draw him away from the rails.

But he continued to stare off into the cold of the lonely sea and sky, where a part of him – and a part of me – would forever be lost.

"The dead don't rest on Toad Hill," my father had said, and I believed him.

They still say the lighthouse is haunted.

Some people talk now of a girl who wanders the rocks at the shore, sometimes smiling sorrowfully at the ocean and other times giggling with a sweetness that makes them ache inside.

She turns her face to the glowing moon, arms outstretched and hands open, as if she is trying to catch broken promises or rose petals.

The Night Is Yours Alone

Michael Rowe

for Angie Moneva

Terry Winter felt sweat soaking though his shirt, prickling his shoulders, carving a narrow trench of wetness down the middle of his back. His stomach churned, and he was aware of a terror so profound it seemed as all-encompassing as white noise on a television set. Mrs. Ritchie's loud, dry voice reading *Great Expectations* to the class, the occasional bored squeak of a chair, the distant shouting on the playing field on the other side of the plate-glass windows – all of these sounds seemed a million miles away. They were no match for the thudding of Terry's heart or the sound of the blood pounding in his ears. His world had been reduced to the sight of the clock on the wall. It was 3:25 p.m. School let out at 3:30 p.m. He would be dead by 3:35 p.m. unless he could run really, really fast.

The distance between the door of the homeroom classroom and the door of the bus – specifically, the seat directly behind the bus driver – could be covered, at a fast run, in three minutes and forty-four seconds. Terry knew this because he had timed it once. As Mrs. Ritchie's favorite, he could exit the classroom the second the bell rang. By running down the hallway as fast as he could – past the locker bay, making a hard left at the cafeteria – he could reach the swinging doors just as Mark Greavy and Jason Doolan were pushing their way to the homeroom door, grunting and red-faced with murderous rage.

Terry suspected that Mrs. Ritchie knew what Greavy and Doolan liked to do to him when they caught him. Although she had never actually heard them use their favorite words – queerboy, faggot, Mrs. Winter, gaylord – Mrs. Ritchie had an uncanny ability to read Terry's body language, or Greavy and Doolan's, and she always seemed to know when after-school violence was being planned. On these afternoons, she somehow saw to it that Greavy and Doolan were the last to leave the classroom, whether she contrived to talk to them about their homework or just made sure that they left the classroom "in an orderly fashion." It gave Terry something like a head start.

Greavy had loudly challenged Mrs. Ritchie on this point one rainy afternoon – and had spent an hour in the office as a result. Mrs. Ritchie had been a teacher since God saw his first ice-cream cake, and the ramrod-stiff, gray-haired lady had little time for attitude or lip from her students. Even the other teachers called Mrs. Ritchie the Iron Maiden behind her back. She'd lived in Auburn her whole life, and when she had graduated from teacher's college, she'd come back to Auburn to teach at the same school she'd attended as a girl (though it was difficult to imagine Mrs. Ritchie having ever been young enough to be called a girl).

Terry had enjoyed his reprieve that Wednesday afternoon, but by Friday, his arms – below the shoulder and above the wrists – were black and blue. He wore long sleeves all the next week, even donning a long-sleeved T-shirt in gym class.

Greavy, like most accomplished bullies, knew how to inflict the maximum pain without leaving marks that adults could easily spot. He also knew that there was no way a little faggot like Terry Winter was going to tell.

The bell rang. Terry heard (or imagined he heard) a triumphant snort from the back of the class, followed by the sound of two chairs scraping away from two desks and two heavy bodies lumbering to life. He felt, rather than saw, the crowd behind him part for Greavy and Doolan, and he felt them coming toward him. He was dimly aware of Mrs. Ritchie shouting at Doolan to slow down, but he knew that even in the unlikely event that Doolan did slow down, Greavy would still get him.

Terry bolted from his seat and lurched toward the door, hip-checked it open, and tumbled into the corridor.

"Excuse me!" he said urgently as he pushed past the students spilling out of the classrooms on either side of his homeroom. "Comin' through! Excuse me!" Then, louder, "Move!"

Behind him, he distinctly heard Doolan shout, "Hey, stop that faggot!" and he heard the sound of ugly, delighted laughter.

Terry ran faster.

"Hey, watch it, for Christ's sake!" someone shouted as Terry jostled through the crowd in blind panic. Ahead of him, the crowd parted momentarily as the front door swung open. Terry caught glorious sight of the afternoon sunlight and the blue fall sky gleaming though the open doorway, and he caught a flash of the yellow school bus. Safety, he thought and closed his eyes in relief.

Just then, he collided with something large and soft. The force of the impact knocked him momentarily off balance, and he slipped on the freshly mopped floor, crashing to the ground, arms flailing and books flying everywhere. He heard a gasp and another thud.

Opening his eyes, Terry saw Mr. Huctwith sprawled against the lockers where he had knocked him. The principal's briefcase was open, and his papers were strewn the length of the corridor.

A small crowd had gathered around them. When Terry heard a girl's squealing laughter behind him and saw the expression on Mr. Huctwith's face turn from disbelief to embarrassment to anger, he knew he was in terrible, terrible trouble.

"Mr. Winter, what do you think you're doing?" Mr. Huctwith snapped. "What is the meaning of this? Why are you running in the corridors?"

"I'm sorry, sir," Terry stuttered. "I . . . I . . . didn't want to miss my bus, sir." He glanced around him, looking for Greavy and Doolan, but he couldn't see either of them.

"The buses don't leave for ten more minutes, and even if they were leaving right now, that wouldn't be any excuse for your behavior." Mr. Huctwith rose unsteadily to his feet, wincing as he did. "I think you and I ought to have a little chat in the office, Mr. Winter."

"But, sir, my bus . . ." Terry's voice cracked and went up a notch. He sounded like a girl at that moment, and he knew it. He also knew that if Mr. Huctwith hadn't been standing there, someone would have told him that he sounded like one. Tears welled up in his eyes. "I need to get home. My . . . my mother needs me," Terry stuttered.

"Well, that's something you should have thought of before you raced through the school. You can explain to your mother why you weren't on the bus this afternoon. Or would you prefer that I telephoned her from the office and told her myself? Yes? No? What?"

Terry shook his head no.

"Come with me," puffed Mr. Huctwith. "I've had just about enough of the flagrant disrespect for rules in this school. This is the last straw, young man."

Terry got to his feet. A bolt of pain shot through his left knee as he stood up. At best, he'd have a hell of a bruise. At worst, he wouldn't be able to run. As he limped down the hallway after Mr. Huctwith, the crowd of students parted to let them through. And then, to his horror, he heard a familiar voice.

"Hi, Terry," Greavy called out softly. "Don't worry, we'll see you get home all right. We'll wait till you're finished with Mr. Huctwith."

"Don't you have someplace to go, Mr. Greavy?" Mr. Huctwith said irritably. "School is out, and I'd rather not have you as my responsibility for one second longer than I have to. It's hard enough keeping you on school property when you're supposed to be here, never mind getting rid of you when you're not."

"Oh, we are just waiting for our friend Terry," Greavy said innocently. "We want to walk home with him this afternoon."

"Yeah, we'll be waiting for you, Winter," Doolan promised. His face was alive with cruelty and anticipation.

How do adults never see this? Terry screamed silently. How does this happen right under their eyes, and they don't even see it? How?

You don't tell them, that's how, a more reasonable voice in his head replied. How can adults do anything if you don't tell them why Doolan and Greavy beat you up, why they hate you so much? Why don't you tell Mr. Huctwith what your secret is? Maybe he could help.

I can't tell anyone! I can't! I can't!

Doolan brushed his knuckle gently against Terry's arm as

he walked by, and Terry remembered the last beating. He thought for a moment that he might throw up, but he didn't.

Terry stared in his bedroom mirror and tried to see himself the way others did. It wasn't hard. He saw a thin-faced boy with pale skin, dark hair, and blue eyes who had often been mistaken for a girl when he was younger. His eyes were puffy and red from crying, and even to Terry, they looked unutterably sad.

He held up his hands and studied his long, slender fingers. He loved to write poetry. He loved to draw, and his room was scattered with his drawings. His grandmother had once told him that his hands were beautiful. An artist's hands, she'd called them. Terry lit a scented candle, switched out the lights in his room, and turned up his CD player so his parents wouldn't hear him crying. The longest nights always began like this, alone and friendless in the silence of his bedroom, the darkness wrapped around him like a warm blanket.

When Terry had come home from school, he'd hidden his torn shirt by keeping his jacket on until he was able to get upstairs to change it. He'd looked in the mirror and seen the new bruises on his upper arms. In a few hours, they would bloom against his skin like angry grape blue flowers, rising vividly out of the fleshy bed of older, yellowing ones. His face had been flushed, and there was a scratch near his eye where Greavy had rubbed his face in the grass. There must have been a sharp rock in there somewhere – a small one, though, because Terry hadn't felt it cut him.

After they'd reduced him to screams by punching his arms in the same place again and again, they'd chased Terry though a muddy field near a subdivision. By the time he'd reached home, his new shoes had been caked in wet mud and clay. His feet felt unbearably heavy, like they were encased in concrete, and he could barely lift them. When his mother saw his ruined shoes, she was furious. She demanded to know who had chased him and why. She wanted to call the culprit's mother and have her pay for the shoes. When Terry refused to tell, insisting that no one had chased him, she called him a liar. He held fast to his story. He knew that if his mother called Mrs. Greavy or Mrs. Doolan, any dream he had of a normal life at school would be gone.

At dinner, his mother had barely spoken to him and his father had kept his eyes on his plate, as though the very sight of Terry was embarrassing to him. Before they'd all sat down at the table, Terry had heard his parents shouting in the kitchen. He knew it was about him. It always was.

In his room that night, he pushed his face deep into his pillow and sobbed, his aching shoulders heaving and falling. Terry had learned years ago that the best way to hide his crying was to lean into the pillow and let it bear some of the weight for him as he wept. It muffled the sound somehow.

He hated himself. He hated the fact that he was . . . *different*. While the other boys were beginning to show an interest in girls, the thought of them filled Terry with a vague, confusing discomfort. Although his friends at his old school had almost exclusively been girls, he had no interest in dating them, and preferred instead to stay in his room and draw or listen to music. He couldn't bring himself to use the ugly words that Doolan and Greavy used to describe him, but he suspected they were true. The words burned him, but there was a cruel truth to them that stabbed him in the chest like nails.

Madonna's music soared from the speakers like a dark bird. The music soothed him, and he didn't doubt for a moment that Madonna would have understood exactly how he felt. The Material Girl had fought her own battles for being different, and she'd won them too. His wall was plastered with her posters, and he owned all her CDs. Terry adored her. Girl music, the kids at school called it. No better than Britney Spears or Mariah Carey. Boys don't listen to music like that. Not normal boys, anyway. Not at this school. Boys listen to Eminem.

In the darkness of his room, Terry felt his sobs finally subside, like they always did. He blew out the candle, switched off his CD player, and drifted off to sleep, his cheek pressed against the damp pillow. In his dreams, he wasn't alone, wasn't different. In his dreams, he had a friend who understood him and liked him exactly as he was.

Terry first saw the boy through the window of the bus the next afternoon after school. He looked to be about thirteen, was skinny, with shaggy blond hair, and was dressed in a pair of very dark blue jeans and a striped T-shirt that looked somehow old-fashioned. As Terry stared through the window of the bus, the kid suddenly turned and looked directly at him, smiled, and waved.

The movement was so abrupt that Terry pulled back as though he'd been burned. He knew it was impossible that the blond boy had seen him staring. The kid was simply too far away to see through the dirty glass of the bus windows.

Terry dared another look. The boy was still standing there. He smiled again, and Terry saw his mouth move, forming Terry's name. It was impossible to hear the kid over the sound of the bus engines and the other kids laughing and talking, but he seemed to be shouting at him, waving frantically. Terry saw people pass by the kid on either side, but no one seemed to be taking any notice. Terry knelt in his seat and pressed his face against the glass of the window. The kid grew smaller and smaller as the bus pulled away.

Who was he? Terry wondered, sitting down in his seat. He'd never seen the kid before, and no one at the school had ever waved at him with that level of enthusiasm, ever. He wished the kid had chosen to wave at him during recess or lunch or gym, so that he could have gone over and talked to him. Terry thought of his strange clothing. He looked a little like a nerd – or at least that's what Greavy and Doolan would have said. And he looked a little frail. Definitely bully bait. Maybe that's why the kid hadn't talked to Terry in school. He had to be new, and he probably didn't want to get lumped in with a loser like Terry Winter so early in the school year.

But it wasn't early – it was late October, almost Halloween.

And if the kid was new, how had he known Terry's name to call it out as the bus pulled away?

"You're quiet tonight," his mother said, helping herself to more potatoes. It was just her and Terry at dinner. His father was bowling. "You haven't said a word since you came home, and you've barely touched anything on your plate. Are you feeling all right?"

"Yeah," Terry said. "Something funny happened today after school. Something weird, in a way."

"Oh no, Terry," his mother said. "Not again. Not those bullies. When are you going to find a way to get along with the other kids?"

"Mom, it wasn't anything like that," Terry said irritably. "Why do you always think it's something bad every time? And always my fault?"

"Because I have some *very* expensive shoes in the basement," his mother replied testily, "that were almost completely *ruined* by a certain *someone* running through a field because he was being chased."

"Mom, that wasn't my fault!" Terry said, raising his voice.

"Well, why were they chasing you, Terry? Why is it that you *always* get chased? Because I'll tell you right now, young man, it takes two to tango. Maybe you should spend less time in your room listening to your music and drawing," she added with disgust, "and more time out in the fresh air, trying to make some friends! Trying to act like a normal, healthy boy instead of some dreamer!"

"Mom –"

"I should call the mothers of those two young men and give them a piece of my mind!" his mother fumed, ignoring Terry. "Those shoes cost me *good money*!"

Terry banged the table with both fists as hard as he could. The silverware and glasses rattled, and the spoon fell out of the bowl of mashed potatoes, clattering onto the kitchen floor.

"Why don't you listen to me?" he screamed. "Why don't you ever hear what I tell you? It's not me! It's not my fault! They don't like me! No one does! They hate everything about me, and they call me terrible, terrible names! They beat me up, and they steal my stuff, and every day is horrible for me. You don't know what it's like here in this town. I wish we'd never moved here. I hate it here. I wish I was dead!"

Terry was shaking. He looked down at his mother. Her face was white, and for once she seemed more shocked than angry or disappointed.

"And I hate you!" he shouted, bursting into tears. "I hate you!"

Terry turned and ran out of the kitchen. He slammed the back door open and took off down the alley behind the house.

Weeping as he ran, he reached the end of the alley and turned left off Webster and onto Sycamore Street. He ran through the subdivision till he got to the edge of the fields near downtown. Slowing, Terry walked through the center of Auburn. Main Street was deserted, the usually inviting storefront windows lit from below. His breath was coming evenly now, mixed with his sobs. He looked up Main Street and headed for the old part of town, and the park that lay beyond it.

Terry was a long way from home, but the thought filled him with comfort rather than unease. After twenty minutes, he passed the cemetery and arrived at Abermarle Avenue. The park was at the end of the street. It was a chilly night, and Terry shivered. An autumn wind had picked up, tossing maple leaves in a spiral dance as they blew through the air. Above him, the moon was almost full and bright white. He began to walk toward the park.

Suddenly, Terry stopped in his tracks and squinted. In the gloom, he could just make out a dim figure sitting atop one of the picnic tables near the edge of the maple trees by the swings.

Was it Greavy or Doolan?

Wouldn't that just be perfect on this horrible night? Terry thought miserably. Wouldn't that just make the whole horrible picture complete? They can chase me through another field, and Mom can call their parents and yell at them. Then they can beat the crap out of me tomorrow at school, but not before they tell everybody that my mom fights my battles for me.

But it wasn't Greavy, and it wasn't Doolan. A shaft of moonlight fell on the figure and glinted off blond hair. Terry walked a little faster. The figure turned to face him, and Terry saw that it was the kid from that afternoon by the buses.

"Hey," Terry called out softly. For some reason, he was

suddenly happier than he ever remembered being. The blond boy was wearing the same striped T-shirt and dark jeans as earlier. His slender arms glowed white in the moonlight. Terry wondered that the kid wasn't freezing. He was dressed for summer, and the park seemed colder than the street, almost as though the temperature had dropped a couple of degrees in the time it had taken him to walk up to the picnic table. The boy seemed oblivious to the chill. His face was very pale, and his eyes were very blue. As he turned his head, his eyes seemed to flicker like a gas fire. Terry felt slightly dizzy for a moment, but the sensation passed as quickly as it came.

Then the boy smiled at him. Terry felt a fluttering in his stomach, and he thought, What a beautiful smile. "What's your name?" he asked.

"Geof," the boy replied softly. He ran a hand across his face and brushed a lock of hair out of his eyes. "With a *g* and one *f*."

"I'm Terry. I live over there." He gestured in the distance with his right arm. "Over on Webster. It's one of the new houses, the ones in the subdivision they just put up."

"I know," Geof said. "I know where you live, and I know what your name is."

"How?" Terry asked, puzzled. "I've never seen you before, and you know my name? How?"

Geof shrugged. "I just do. I saw you on the bus today. I've tried to get your attention before, but you've been too far away to hear me, I guess."

"You mean today, right? Out by the buses?"

"Yeah, today for sure. Some other times as well. It doesn't really matter."

"Do you go to our school?"

"I used to. I just came back to visit today. My mom still lives around here. I came to see her too."

"Do you live with your dad?"

Geof shrugged again. "No, but it doesn't matter. Hey," he said, reaching out and putting his hand on Terry's shoulder, "how come you've been crying? Trouble with your mom?"

"How did you know that?" Terry was surprised. "My mom and I had a fight. We seem to fight a lot these days."

"What did you fight about?"

"You wouldn't understand." Terry felt tears gathering again, and for a moment, his vision blurred. The street lamps in the park swam in a halo of light, and the figure of Geof shimmered and became insubstantial. Terry wiped his eyes with the back of his hand. "Nobody would."

"Try me," Geof said. "What have you got to lose?"

Terry took a deep breath. "I'm . . . uh, I'm not like a lot of other guys," he said hesitantly. He paused, then went on. "I'm different." Terry suddenly felt light-headed. I've never said that to another person in my life, he thought giddily. And it feels so good to say it.

"It's good, sometimes, to say these things out loud, isn't it?" Geof said kindly. "You just need to find someone to say them to. That's the trick."

Terry's jaw dropped. It was as though the boy had read his mind.

"And it's all right to be different," he added. "That's not a *problem*, man. That's just *life*. A lot of guys aren't like a lot of other guys."

"My mom wishes I was," Terry said, sighing.

"Parents," Geof said, with some humor. "Sometimes they understand about stuff, sometimes they don't. It's not their fault, really. They forget the way they were at our age."

"What do you know about it?" Terry said glumly. "My life sucks. My parents hate me. I don't have any friends. People beat me up all the time. I can't see it ever getting better. Sometimes I think the best thing would be to kill myself. It would make it all a lot easier. My parents would be sorry, and Greavy and Doolan – they're the guys who beat me up and call me names – they'd get in so much trouble. It would make things a lot easier."

"No, it wouldn't," Geof said quietly. "You don't want to do that, trust me. That's not any kind of a solution."

"Why not?" Terry said defiantly. "Give me one good reason."

"Well, for one thing, it would be boring as hell to be dead, don't you think?" Geof threw back his head and laughed. The sound was full of joy, like music to Terry's ears, and he suddenly found himself unable to keep from laughing too. It seemed like the funniest thing he had ever heard.

Then Geof's laughter stopped, and he looked at Terry strangely. "And," he said, serious again, "even if it wouldn't be boring as hell to be dead, you have a lot of things to do before you get there."

"Like what?" Terry asked. He felt the sadness returning. The night beyond the street lamps and the park seemed suddenly very cold and black. He caught the whiff of autumn earth from the fields beyond the town, and in the distance, he heard the lonely whine of a long-haul truck barreling down the highway. "What do I have to do?"

"Terry," Geof said earnestly, "this isn't *it*, you know." He waved his arm, taking in the park, the houses, the twinkling lights of Auburn glittering over the dark hills of the escarpment that encircled the town. "This is just a waystation. A stopover. Every day that you have to get up and go to that school, and face those people and listen to the things they say, it may seem like this is your life. But it's not. Your life will be what you make of it later. And there's so much you can do with it. You have so much work to do in life, and so many people to love and so many people who'll love *you*. There's so much beauty in you, Terry. You may not see it yet, but you will, and so will other people. They're not all like the people here. There's a world out there beyond Auburn, and you have a wonderful place in it. Your life is a tapestry, Terry, and you're the one who embroiders it. You, and nobody else. Choose your own colors and make it brilliant and beautiful."

"You don't know what it's like having bullies chase you all the time, being called names and getting beaten up. You have no idea."

"Yes, I do," Geof said gently. "I know a thing or two about that. I've met a few bullies in my time."

"How the hell do you know all of this stuff?" Terry asked belligerently. "*Your* time? You're not any older than I am. You don't know anything about what it's like to be me or live in my shoes. I know you mean well, but this is just smoke. Life is a tapestry? Give me a break. Why the hell am I even talking to you about this? I have to get home."

Geof suddenly jumped off the picnic table, put his hands on Terry's shoulders, and shook him gently. "Look at me," he commanded, and Terry did.

It was as though he had been dropped into a vacuum. There was no sound and no air, but somehow he could breathe. He heard nothing but the sound of his heart beating and the rush of his blood. He stared into Geof's flickering blue eyes. He couldn't look away, didn't want to. He felt like he was floating over a beautiful sunstruck landscape of bright warm colors and sweet, sweet singing. He knew, suddenly, that things wouldn't always be the way they were right now. He knew that things would change for him. He knew that he was loved, and that he would be loved later, across the years.

He knew he was treasured. Infinite possibility seemed to sweep before him like an empty silver highway.

"How do you know?" Terry whispered dizzily. "How do you know all of this?" He heard the sound of his own voice as though it was a million miles away, as though it was coming from the moon.

"I just do, Terry. You have to trust me on this one." Geof released his shoulders and looked away, breaking their eye contact.

Terry felt as though he had been struck by lightning. He looked around him. The hardness of the pavement beneath, the sharply etched outlines of the picnic table, the fluorescent street lamps, the ugly edges of the subdivision houses half draped in shadow, the sounds of a town at night – they all seemed unbearably loud and ugly compared with the world he'd imagined a second before. He crossed his arms across his chest and shivered. "What happened just now?" he asked desperately. "What happened? What did you do to me?"

"Nothing." Geof shrugged. "I didn't do anything at all. We were just talking." He smiled crookedly at Terry. "Why? Did something happen that I missed? Are you feeling better?"

"Yeah, I am," Terry said, surprised. "I am feeling better. I don't know why, but I am." He looked down at his watch and sighed. "I've got to get home. My mom is gonna kill me. I have a curfew." He turned and began walking out of the park.

"I doubt she'll kill you over that." Geof laughed. "It hasn't been that long. Go on home."

"What about you?" Terry called over his shoulder. "Don't you have a curfew?"

Geof had stepped back from the picnic table and was standing in the shadows of the maple trees with his hands in his pockets. Terry squinted, but he could barely make him out in the darkness.

"I've got to get going too," Geof said. He began walking in the opposite direction, deeper into the park, toward the trees. "It's late."

Terry stopped. "Will I see you at school tomorrow?" It suddenly seemed very important to him that he see his new friend again soon. "Will I see you after school, at least?"

"Maybe," Geof's voice floated across the park. "I'm around. I'll keep an eye out for you."

"Great!" Terry said. "See you!" He sprinted for the street, then suddenly remembered that he hadn't asked Geof for his phone number or found out where he lived. He turned around and opened his mouth to call out his new friend's name, then stopped in his tracks.

The park was empty. The trees cast wildly twisting phantom shadows on the green-black moon-dappled grass as they blew in the autumn wind. Dry leaves flew through the black night air, vanishing into the deeper black beyond the circle of streetlight.

The next afternoon, Terry decided to walk home. He was hoping he would run into Geof again, and he stayed back when the others lined up and boarded the big yellow buses in front of the school.

Greavy and Doolan hadn't been in class that day. Both of them had called in sick. Terry didn't believe for a second that either of them was anything but healthy, but the joy of a day without their reign of terror was such a gift that he didn't think about it more than in passing. The final bell had rung at the usual time, and Terry had stepped out into the corridor without the dread that usually accompanied him like an indoor shadow.

He scanned the crowd outside the school. Geof had said he was just visiting, but if he came by school once, he might do so again, even if it was just to say good-bye before he went back home. For the first time since he could remember, Terry didn't feel so alone. And in not feeling so alone, he didn't feel quite as afraid.

It was weird the way his imagination had taken flight while he was talking to Geof, and the haunting visions had followed him home. That night, he'd dreamed as much as he always did, but he'd dreamed he was older. He didn't live in Auburn – he lived in the city, and he had a job and friends. He was in love, and he loved as well.

He'd woken up to yellow fall sunlight coming through his bedroom window, and he had lain in bed for a few minutes, warm under the covers, smiling as he tried to catch the waves of joy that lingered from his dream. Even his mother had sensed that his mood had shifted, and she was puzzled. She'd asked him what he was so happy about at the breakfast table. He'd just smiled and told her he'd had a good sleep.

Terry was disappointed when the last bus pulled away and the crowd of students dwindled. Geof was nowhere to be seen. He sighed and picked up his knapsack. He strolled over to the library to see if Geof was there, but he wasn't. Terry next checked the gym. There was a basketball practice going on, and he stayed close to the wall to avoid getting in the way. He looked up at the bleachers, but all he could see was a scattering of the basketball players' girlfriends and a couple of parents. No Geof. He checked the auditorium. Nobody there but the choir members, practicing for their mid-November Handel recital.

Deeply disappointed, Terry headed for home. He decided that he would go back to the park after dinner and see if Geof was waiting for him there. He'd felt a strong connection to the strange blond boy, and he didn't believe that night would be the last time they'd ever meet.

What had Geof said? "Your life is a tapestry . . . you're the one who embroiders it." How would he embroider *his* tapestry, he mused. What was he good at? He loved to draw, and he loved music. He knew there was a world out there where these things were valued. He'd read about that world in books and magazines, and he'd seen it on television. Maybe that was his place. Maybe Geof was right. Maybe all of this *was* just a stopover. He began to whistle.

"Well, well, well," Greavy said as he came around the corner. "It's Mrs. Winter." A cigarette hung crookedly from his lip. Behind him, Doolan slouched against the wall. He too was smoking.

Doolan took the cigarette out of his mouth and flicked it onto the sidewalk, grinding it out with the tip of his steel-toed workboot. He flexed his fingers and curled them into fists, then walked over to Greavy and draped his arm over his shoulder. The two stared at Terry wolfishly. He marveled at how easy it was to read their minds. All they seemed to enjoy was inflicting pain. He'd never seen anything on their faces but a savage, stupid delight at the thought of making Terry scream. He didn't know why they hated him, but he knew they did.

"What are you doing here, faggot?" Greavy growled. "Are you waitin' for us?"

He said the first thing that came to his mind. "I thought you were sick today."

"We *are* sick, queerboy," Doolan sneered. "We're sick of seeing your pathetic face every day. So maybe we should fix that right now. Whaddaya say, Greavy? Huh? Shall we fix Mrs. Winter one last time?"

Greavy reached out and shoved Terry, hard. He flew

against the wall, striking his head on the brick. He saw a bright flash of light, then a shower of stars as he fell to the ground, stunned. His books had fallen out of his knapsack, and as he watched, Greavy drew back his booted foot and kicked them as hard as he could. Papers flew in every direction, fluttering down around Terry like wounded birds.

"Get up, queerboy," Greavy grunted. "Get up and fight like a man."

No dreams for me, he thought. No joy. This is it. This is my life. And then he remembered Geof's promise of a world where he would someday shine, and something snapped.

Without thinking, Terry leapt to his feet and shouted as loud as he could, "Why do you do this to me, you guys? What have I ever done to you? Nothing! I've never done anything to either of you, and you make my life a living hell *every day*! Why? What's your problem?"

Greavy and Doolan took an involuntary step back, a look of dull surprise crossing their faces. Terry took a step forward, and Doolan and Greavy took another step back.

"You think you're tough?" Terry shouted. "How would you know? Have you ever hit someone who could hit you back, harder? You know I can't protect myself, and that's why you do it! I'm smaller than you are, and I can't fight! I wouldn't want to anyway, even if I could, because it's stupid! Every day you beat me up. You chase me though fields. You call me names. You're not ever happy unless I'm bruised or bleeding or crying. Fine. You want to beat me up? Go for it! Knock my teeth out. Kill me if you want to. But I'll tell you this." Terry leaned forward and shoved his index finger in Doolan's face and shook it. "It doesn't prove anything except that you're a couple of damn cowards. And I'm sick of it, so if you want to finish me off, just try to do it right now! I may wind up in the hospital, but I'll make sure that you two wind up in jail for a long, long time. And I'll tell the newspapers about what really happened, and everyone will know what a couple of loser cowards you really are. Now go to hell!"

He was shaking, and his heart was pounding harder than he could ever remember. He turned his back on Doolan and Greavy, who looked at each other in stunned silence, then began glancing around to see if anyone else had heard Terry's outburst. They looked at Terry blankly, like animals whose dinner had been snatched away from them by some magic they didn't understand.

Terry bent down and began picking up his torn papers and books and putting them back into his knapsack. He was still afraid of Doolan and Greavy, but he knew that if they touched him, he'd do some damage of his own. What's the worst thing they can do? he thought. Hurt me? I've been hurt plenty. I already know what pain feels like. If they don't know what it feels like, I'll find some way to show them.

"What on earth is going on back here?" a voice snapped. It was Mrs. Ritchie. "I *demand* an explanation for this shouting. *At once*!" She had come around the corner and was standing in front of them, holding a folder of tests she was taking home to correct. Terry remembered that she often stayed behind after school to tutor students.

Mrs. Ritchie surveyed the scene. Her eyes skimmed over Terry's torn books and papers and lingered there. She glanced at him with sympathy, but it was mixed with something else. Terry watched the fury grow. Her mouth tightened. When she looked over at Greavy and Doolan, her eyes were blazing.

"Mr. Greavy," she said coldly, "Mr. Doolan. Shall I tell you a little secret, gentlemen? I've always rather suspected that you two are bound for jail. In fact, Mr. Huctwith and I were discussing that in the teachers' lounge this afternoon. I think you're in the process of proving me right, and at a very comfortable pace. I thank you for that."

"We weren't doin' nothin', ma'am," Doolan said sullenly. "You didn't see us do nothin'."

"Terry!" Greavy snorted. "Hey, buddy! Tell Mrs. Ritchie that we were just foolin' around. We're buddies."

Terry said nothing. He resumed picking up his books and papers.

"Be quiet," Mrs. Ritchie said in a voice like a whip. "How dare you address me in that tone of voice! Mr. Huctwith will deal with your delinquency today – claiming to be ill when you clearly aren't. But I promise you, I will take a personal interest in this bullying incident, which I know, by the way, is far from an isolated one. By the time I'm finished with the two of you for this . . . this outrage, you'll be begging for me to have you expelled!" She took a step forward. "You were going to beat this young man, and I know why too. Do you know what a hate crime is? It's what this type of bullying is called in the real world. I may be limited in the punishment I can inflict upon you, but I assure you that I will see to it that this *never* happens again." Her face was chalk white except for two angry red spots on each cheek.

Terry saw something he never expected to see as he gazed at his tormentors. They were terrified. So this is what I look like when they look at me, he thought. This is what it looks like when the shoe is on the other foot. He felt a twinge of pity in spite of himself.

"Now get home!" Mrs. Ritchie shouted. "I'll deal with you two tomorrow, and if you're not out of here in two minutes, I will have you arrested for trespassing on school property after hours. *Go!*"

Doolan and Greavy took off running across the playground.

"Are you all right, Terry?" Mrs. Ritchie said kindly. "Did they hit you?"

"Not this time," Terry said quietly. He zipped up his knapsack and slung it over his shoulder.

"Terry," said Mrs. Ritchie, "I heard what you said to those two, and I want you to know I'm very proud of you for standing up for yourself. I know it's not easy when you're the one people choose to pick on. They say you're different, and they use that as an excuse to beat you up. Well, you know what? That's never an excuse."

"Then why do they do it?" Terry said angrily. "Why?"

"Right now, in junior high, and later, in high school, you'll find that everyone wants everyone else to be the same as them. Anyone different or original or unique makes them nervous. It's just their own fear of not fitting in themselves."

"Why should anybody be afraid of me? I don't get it."

"Because you're different from them, Terry, and they sense it," Mrs. Ritchie said. "You're special. You care about things other than the things they care about. You have talents, and you're unique. That's wonderful. It's the different ones who wind up making the difference in the world." She paused. "Do you understand what I'm saying to you, Terry? You have some wonderful gifts. I've seen your drawings. You're special. Special people are often *very, very* different from others. It comes with the territory."

"I don't want to be special; I want to be *normal*!" he said desperately. "I want to be like everyone else!"

"Oh, Terry, don't *ever* wish for that!" Mrs. Ritchie laughed. "Normal is *highly* overrated. It may seem like that's what you want right now, and I don't blame you. But don't forget that someday none of this will matter, and when the world knows who you are, you'll look back at these days and laugh." She paused, then added seriously, "Well, even if you don't laugh, you'll think you did a good thing by surviving them." Her face darkened. "Some don't."

"What do you mean?" Terry asked.

"Oh." Mrs. Ritchie sighed. "It doesn't really matter, Terry."

He reached out and plucked at the sleeve of her coat. "Please, Mrs. Ritchie. Tell me. I need to know."

She looked down at him and her face softened. "All right, I'll tell you," she said reluctantly. "I had a student once, a long time ago. It was 1957, in fact. He was a wonderful boy, very intelligent. He was gentle and kind, and he loved to paint. He painted some beautiful pictures."

"What happened to him?"

"He used to get picked on," she said. "Terribly. They beat him up, and they called him names. In fact," she said, with private anger, "Mark Greavy's father was one of the worst offenders. I'm not surprised to see his son carrying on the family tradition."

"Didn't anyone try to catch them? To stop them?" Terry asked. "Couldn't they see what was happening?"

"I was a young teacher then," Mrs. Ritchie replied. "In those days, nobody cared about bullying. Today we understand that the kids who bully others often go on to do some pretty horrible things in later life, and we try to stop it when we can. But in 1957, people used to say that it was just a normal part of growing up, and the popular wisdom was to let the children work it out among themselves." She shuddered. "Well, there's nothing *normal* about it," she said bitterly. "It can have dreadful consequences."

"Mrs. Ritchie," Terry whispered urgently, "*what happened to the boy?*"

"He killed himself," she said shortly. "One night, he just decided that he'd had enough. He got his mother's sleeping pills and took the whole bottle." Her eyes grew moist, and she looked away. "God knows what kind of a life he could have had. He could have been anything he wanted to be. He was like you, Terry," she said, kneeling down and peering into his face. "There was a light in him. He was special, and so are you. Never forget that. No matter how bad things get right now, don't do anything stupid."

Terry stared at her. "That's so sad," he said.

"It was," she agreed. Then, briskly, she said, "Let's go to the office. I think we'll arrange to have you sent home in a taxi. I don't think Mr. Greavy and Mr. Doolan are foolish enough to try anything this evening, but why risk it?"

As they entered the school building, Terry stopped at the class pictures hanging on the wall. They stretched back all the way to 1932, the year the school had opened. He scrutinized the photographs behind the glass, smudged as they were by years of chalk dust and age. Then he glanced at Mrs. Ritchie with a curious expression on his face.

"Mrs. Ritchie," he said, running his fingers across the pictures. "Did you say 1957?"

"What? I'm sorry, Terry," she replied. She stopped walking and looked back at Terry, who was now studying the photographs intently. "What did you say?"

"The boy," he said. "Your student. The one you were talking about. The one who . . . well, the one who died. Is he up here on the wall?"

She looked at Terry long and hard, as though weighing something in her mind. Then she walked over to one of the group photographs and tapped her finger against the grimy glass.

"This is him," she said quietly. "And this is the last time I want to talk about any of this, Terry. Ever. This has nothing to do with you or your life. Do we understand each other?"

"Yes, ma'am," he replied, his back turned to Mrs. Ritchie as he stared at the boy in the yellowed black-and-white photograph. The boy's hair was obviously blond and shaggy. He was dressed in a striped T-shirt that had probably not looked old-fashioned in 1957. He had a beautiful smile. Terry looked down at the name under the photograph

Geoffrey Edgar Person.

He'd found Geof at last – at the end of a darkening hallway on the way to the office, in an old photograph, behind glass. Geoffrey Edgar Person, who would be thirteen forever. Terry wondered how many times he had passed the picture over the course of a day, never stopping to look. There had never been a reason to, after all.

"Geof," he said, in a hushed voice. "It's Geof." He traced his index finger gently across the boy's face. He felt tears rising, but he pushed them down.

"That's what we called him," Mrs. Ritchie said quietly. "Geof. 'With a *g* and one *f*,' he always used to say. I remember that part like it was yesterday." She laughed lightly. "Now come on, Terry. Enough is enough. Let's get you that taxi. Your parents will be wondering where you are."

"Mrs. Ritchie?" Terry took a deep breath. "I think I'll pass on the taxi, if it's all right with you. I want to walk home. I'm not afraid of Greavy and Doolan any more. I want to walk."

"Are you sure?" Mrs. Ritchie looked worried. "It's no trouble to call a taxi. Or," she said, glancing down at her watch, "I could drive you home myself."

"I've never been more sure of anything in my life," he said. "I'll see you tomorrow, Mrs. Ritchie."

Terry walked out into the dwindling October light. Shadows were lengthening across the schoolyard as he strode briskly to the street. He zipped up his jacket and tucked his head down against the wind that had sprung up, blowing bits of paper and debris into the air, tasting of winter's killing cold. He turned and took one look back at the school. His eyes traveled across the line of buildings, settling on the playground at the farthest edge of the property.

A blond boy in a striped T-shirt and dark blue jeans sat on the swings. Terry was too far away to see his face, but he didn't have to see it to know that he was smiling. The boy waved once, then he was gone.

"Thank you, Geof," he whispered softly. "Good-bye." He stood there silently for a long time with his head bowed, thinking.

Then he turned and headed into the gathering dusk toward home.

Monster on His Back

Michael Arruda

The girl of his dreams was in front of him.

Dodie Metcalf, the most beautiful girl in the school. The most beautiful-looking creature he had ever laid eyes on.

Behind him, riding on his back and looking over his shoulder, was the monster. The unseen creature who'd been haunting him for months, hounding him ever since he first realized he "liked" Dodie.

She's too good-looking for you, the monster said. *She'll never go out with you!*

"Leave me alone!" Roddy shot back, wading through the congested halls of New Bedford High School. Halls teeming with students, twenty-eight hundred of them, all trying to reach their next class within three minutes.

It was the last day of school, and Dodie would be off to camp for the summer. It was now or never.

He caught up to Dodie and tapped her on the shoulder. "Hi, Dodie!"

She turned her head, her eyes meeting his. "Hi, Roddy," she said with a half-smile.

His knees wobbled. For a moment, he forgot how to breathe. Then, with a flourish, "Missed you yesterday in English!"

Oh, that *was smooth!*

"I stayed home. It's not like we're doing work any more," Dodie said.

"That's true. We're not. Well, I just wanted to say . . . good-bye."

Idiot!

"And . . . um, wish you a good summer."

"Thanks. You have a good summer too."

"Thanks."

He was running out of time. Passing period was nearly over. A sudden drought parched his mouth; his tongue became swollen with a foul coating of anxiety. He couldn't speak.

Cat got your tongue? Heh, heh!

Why was it so difficult? Why did his tongue become a twisted pretzel every time he was with this girl? He wanted to scream. And why was it so loud? All around him, it was like a raucous crowd at a baseball game. How can a guy be expected to pose a romantic question in these surroundings?

He wished he was on a soap opera. Those guys had it easy. Wanna ask your dream girl out? Soap opera guy would have an entire restaurant reserved just for him and his woman, with hundreds of lit candles in the background and romantic music softly supporting his every word. The surroundings would be so quiet that he could whisper and she'd still hear everything he had to say.

What did he have?

A school corridor filled to capacity with rowdy teenagers and only thirty seconds to make his pitch. While speed walking.

What chance did he have? What chance did any high-schooler have with a teasing, taunting monster on his back – one that wouldn't let him relax for a second?

Say something! Say it now . . . if you can! the monster roared.

"Dodie, I was wondering – Ow!"

Roddy stumbled backwards, was nearly knocked off his feet by a tall, lanky freshman overexcited about becoming a sophomore. The future basketball star had collided into Roddy, sending him crashing into a locker.

"Why don't you watch where you're going?" Roddy cried.

"Sorry, man!" answered the soon-to-be sophomore, never breaking his stride.

Weakling! Fall on your butt, why don't you?

Roddy rubbed his face in embarrassment, shielding his eyes from Dodie's gaze.

"Are you all right?" she asked and touched his shoulder.

He experienced a sudden surge of strength, brought on by the feel of her slender fingertips.

"Yeah. Freshmen! Anyway, Dodie, I was wondering –"

She looked him right in the eye. Her brown eyes were the most beautiful things he had ever seen.

Look at those eyes. They're perfect! You're out of your league.

"Shut up!"

"Excuse me?" Dodie asked.

"Er . . . nothing. I was wondering if . . . if maybe we'll get a chance . . . Do you think you'd –"

The bell rang.

That's it. Game over!

"Gotta get to class," Dodie said. "See you later."

She walked away.

What a loser.

"Dodie!" he called.

She stopped, turned around.

"Can I just . . . I know the bell rang, but it's the last day of school. Can I ask you something?"

"Sure," she said, approaching him.

Roddy's stomach churned like a flushing toilet and his face blazed like a furnace, dripping sweat down his temples and neck.

She can see you sweating!

He ignored the monster on his back. Ignored it as best he could, even as he knew she could see the embarrassment on his face, the wetness saturating his collar and shirt.

"You were talking about some new movie the other day, and I thought – I don't know – it might be fun if we went to see it together."

"You and me?" Dodie asked, her face brightening with a smile.

"Yeah. But we don't have to or anything, if you're . . . you know, busy."

"When did you want to go?"

"How about tomorrow night?"

"Sure, why not?"

Roddy wasn't sure he'd heard her right. "What?"

"It might be fun." She paused, then said, "Look, I've got to go. We can talk more about this later."

A sense of calm flooded over Roddy, like cool, cool water.

And the monster, it seemed, had nothing to say.

"She said yes!" he shouted. "I'm going out with Dodie Metcalf!"

Big deal, said the monster.

"What are you still doing here?" Roddy asked. "You're supposed to be gone now."

Why?

"I asked her out. She said yes."

No, no. We're just getting started, Roddy, my boy!

"But I thought –"

You thought that if you asked your little cutie for a date, I'd go away? I'd be crushed by your small victory?

"Something like that."

Wrong! the monster snickered. *Tell me, Roddy, on Friday night, on your date, are you going to . . . hold her hand? Kiss her? What if you try and she refuses? Can you handle that? What if you tell a joke, and she doesn't laugh but rolls her eyes instead? What if you can't stop saying the same thing over and over again? What* will *you do?*

Roddy screamed.

And the monster laughed.

Girls' Night Out

Edo van Belkom

Amanda Kelly stood in front of the mirror dressed only in a Riviera blue bra and matching panties. She'd bought them at La Senza at Shopper's World with her own money and just for tonight.

New Year's Eve.

Tonight everything was going to be special.

She turned from side to side, watching herself closely, noticing how the underwear – no, *lingerie* – made her look more like a woman than a girl. She hadn't exactly filled out up top, but she was getting there.

Another six months, maybe a year.

One thing she didn't have to wait for was her legs. They were already long and shapely, and every time she wore a skirt to school, with heels or without, all the boys seemed to notice her. And tonight she was going to show them off, with natural pantyhose and a pair of leather slingbacks with a three-inch heel.

She pulled on the pantyhose, then slid her new black stretch-jersey dress over her head and pulled it down the length of her body. It was made of spandex and clung to her like a second skin. It had a turtleneck, bare arms, and a daring slit up the right side.

Nice.

She adjusted the dress, then slipped into her new heels, being careful not to pull too hard on the thin leather strap that went around the back of her ankle.

Finally, she was dressed and the outfit she had imagined herself going to the party in was complete.

She turned around and around, looking at herself from every angle, liking what she saw.

And she hadn't even put on any makeup yet.

Just then, the phone rang.

"Hello?"

"Hey, Mandy, are you ready?" It was Amanda's best friend, Lucy.

"Girl, I've been ready for weeks. What about you?"

"I can't decide which sweater to wear. They all make me look fat."

"Sweater? You're wearing a *sweater*?" Lucy was such a straight arrow. Sometimes it was a drag, but Amanda really couldn't complain. Her parents had been against her going to the party until they'd learned that Lucy would be going with her. Hearing that, they not only had agreed but were even letting her drive herself to the party in her mother's car, since they were going to a party of their own.

"Yes, a sweater. It's going to be cold out."

"*Hello*, the car does have a heater, you know. It'll even be warm by the time I pick you up."

"Well, I guess I could try a blouse . . ."

"Now you're talking."

"When are you picking me up?"

"I'll be leaving in half an hour."

"Okay, I'll be ready."

"In a blouse, right?" Amanda asked, but Lucy had already hung up the phone.

&

"I'm going now, bye!" Amanda said as she put on her coat. It was a mid-length trench that covered her legs to just below the knee.

"Wait!" her mother called from upstairs, where she and Dad were getting dressed themselves. "I want to see what you look like."

Amanda sighed, knowing that her mother wouldn't approve of what she was wearing, mostly because she'd picked the outfit out herself.

Her mother came down the stairs.

"Oh, no," she said.

"What is it?"

"It's too cold for those shoes. Put on your boots instead."

No way, thought Amanda. Boots would spoil the look.

"They don't go with my dress," she said.

"Then take your shoes with you and change when you get to the party."

Amanda knew it wouldn't do her any good to argue with her mother, so she said, "All right."

"Marilyn," her dad called from upstairs. "Have you seen my snowflake tie?"

"Just a minute, dear," Amanda's mom shouted. She turned to take one last look at her daughter. "You look beautiful." There was real pride in her voice. "Drive carefully."

"Yes, Mom."

"And put on your boots," her mother reminded, then hurried upstairs to help her dad.

When her mother was gone, Amanda extended her right leg so she could see her ankle, foot, and shoe. She twisted her foot around and liked the way the shoe shaped her foot, made it look . . . well, all grown-up. She couldn't possibly put on her boots; it would ruin *everything*.

She tossed her boots in the closet and hurried out the door.

The car's heater was finally blowing hot air by the time Amanda reached Lucy's house. The heat felt good on Amanda's legs, especially because her feet and toes had almost frozen while she'd waited for what seemed like forever for the car to warm up.

She honked twice on the car's horn, not wanting to venture out into the cold. It had begun to snow, and there were a few inches of snow on Lucy's driveway that would make a mess of her new shoes.

She was about to honk again when the front door opened. Lucy's parents waved to Amanda through the storm door, and then Lucy appeared, wearing her usual winter coat, pants, and a pair of – *ugh* – bowling shoes.

"Hey, Amanda," Lucy said when she opened the door.

"Hey, Lucy." She'd tried to keep the disappointment from her voice but failed miserably.

"What's wrong?"

"I don't think we can get a lane tonight on such short notice."

Lucy looked at her feet. "Oh, I decided on the sweater, and these were the only shoes that went with it. They're not really bowling shoes; they just look like it."

Amanda put the car into reverse and backed out of the driveway.

"Wow," Lucy said. "*Your* shoes look great!"

"Thanks. I like them."

"But aren't they a little cold for December?"

Amanda smiled. "No way, girlfriend. These shoes are hot any time of the year."

The two friends laughed.

Later, as Amanda passed the sign marking the city limits, Lucy asked, "You have the invitation?"

"Under your visor."

The party was being held at William Markham's house. He lived outside of town and drove to school in his own car. His father owned some sort of construction company and was supposed to be rich. Even though William lived out in the country, and his place was a little tough to get to, no one was going to miss *his* party. He was on the honor roll, was captain of the football team, and had everything else that went with good looks and money. His party was the place to be on New Year's Eve, and *everybody* was going to be there.

Lucy took out the invitation and looked over the map and directions printed on the back. "Seems easy enough to get to."

"How hard can it be?" Amanda said. "William drives to school every day."

"Turn here!"

Amanda made a sudden right turn. The rear of the car skidded slightly around the corner, but she was able to maintain control.

"You sure this is it?" she asked. It was a narrow dirt road with trees lining each side and not a single house light anywhere to be seen.

"Pretty sure. It says, 'First right after Rooker Road.'"

Amanda nodded. "Okay, what's next?"

Lucy studied the map. "Not sure."

Amanda slowed and pulled over. "Let me see."

Lucy handed her the map.

The directions had all seemed so easy when she'd looked them over in her kitchen that afternoon. Her father had known where the house was and told her it would be easy to find. Now, with snow falling and no streetlights or markers, it was almost impossible to tell where they were.

"Okay. We just made a right, so we should be here." Amanda pointed to a spot on the map, then read the instructions out loud. "Turn left at the next crossroads and drive straight for ten minutes. The house will be on your right."

"So we have to find the crossroads," Lucy said.

"Haven't crossed anything yet."

"Then let's keep going."

Amanda drove on for several minutes but didn't see any crossroads.

"We didn't pass it, did we?"

"No," Lucy said. "I don't think so. We did pass a road, but that was just one road on the right, and it looked like a driveway. At least, it looked that way through the snow."

They continued on.

"Maybe we should turn back," Lucy said a little while later. "We should have seen a crossroads by now."

Amanda considered turning around but decided to give it another minute or two.

Lucy suddenly jumped up in her seat. "Ah, here it is!"

The crossroads loomed ahead.

Amanda turned right. "Okay. Let me know when ten minutes has passed."

Lucy pulled back her sleeve and stared at her watch.

Sometime later, she said, "That's it. Ten minutes."

Amanda stared out into the darkness but saw nothing but blackness and snow. "Where's the house?"

"It should be on the left."

"No, the right."

Lucy brought out the directions and read them aloud. "Turn left at the next crossroads and drive straight for ten minutes. The house will be on your right." She turned to look at Amanda. "You turned right back there."

"Oops, sorry."

"We have to turn around."

Easier said than done. The road was even narrower here, and with snow piled up on either side, there was barely room for two cars to pass, never mind one car to get turned around.

"Look for a driveway," Amanda said.

But there was none.

Finally, Lucy saw something that they might be able to use. "How about that?" It was a gate that led to a farmer's field. It wasn't plowed, but the ground in front of it was flat enough to pull onto and turn around on.

"It'll have to do."

Amanda slowed to a crawl, then gently eased the car onto the flat spot. As she was about to stop and put the car into reverse, she heard a loud scraping sound coming from under the front end. It sounded a lot like the time she ran over a concrete curb in the Blockbuster parking lot, only this was louder and the car seemed to get hung up on whatever was under the wheels.

Not only that, but the engine had cut out too, leaving the two girls in complete and utter silence.

"What happened?" Lucy cried.

"I think I ran over something."

"Well, start the car and let's get out of here."

Amanda turned the key. There was a sharp click, then nothing.

"Won't start."

"What?"

"I turned the key, but it's dead."

"It has to start," Lucy cried.

Amanda tried again, but now there wasn't even a click.

"What are we going to do now?"

"My father's going to kill me," Amanda said.

"Never mind that. We have to get out of here."

"We can walk," Amanda suggested.

"Which way?"

"Back toward the party."

"Are you crazy? It's a ten-minute drive back to the crossroads, and then another ten minutes to William's house. Do you know how long a walk that is?"

Amanda shrugged.

"It has to be more than ten miles." Lucy looked at Amanda's shoes. "And you're not walking ten feet in those things."

Amanda looked at her shoes – her nice, new grown-up shoes – and felt the first pinch of cold on her toes.

"We could stay here in the car" – she pulled the switch for the hazard lights – "and wait for someone to come by and see us on the side of the road."

"Who's going to come this way when the party's over there?" Lucy pointed in the direction they'd come.

"We went the wrong way, so maybe someone else will too. Or maybe a snowplow?"

"Yeah." Lucy sighed. "Maybe a snowplow, on some narrow dirt road outside of town on New Year's Eve."

Amanda said nothing.

The girls waited in silence, except for the constant tink of hazard lights that steadfastly told the world that here were two girls in trouble.

ɣ

Not a single car passed by in the hour they'd been waiting. Amanda's feet were freezing, and her toes felt as if concrete blocks had been dropped onto them. She'd tried to warm her feet by rubbing them with her hands, but it was like trying to boil an egg with a book of matches. There just wasn't enough heat to get the job done.

Lucy was faring a little better, but her bowling shoes didn't do all that much once the cold had settled in.

"We have to do something," Amanda said. "We just can't stay here and freeze to death."

"We should stay with the car. It's cold, but at least it's protecting us from the wind and snow. And the lights might attract someone's attention."

"All right, then," Amanda said. "I guess we can wait a little while longer."

The car was silent for a few moments, then Lucy said, "You've kissed a boy, haven't you?"

"Two. Joey and Ramone."

"Tell me what it was like . . ."

ɣ

Another hour had passed, and still no sign of anyone.

Amanda rocked back and forth in the driver's seat, trying to think of anything but her cold, cold feet. They weren't cold any more; now it felt more like daggers had been forced through her soles.

Lucy was the first to speak. "We have to do *something*." There was a tone of defeat in her voice.

Amanda tried to keep the tears from her eyes but couldn't. "I thought you said we had to stay with the car."

"I did, but now it's ten o'clock, and for sure there won't be anyone coming by for at least another two hours. I can't wait here that long."

Amanda couldn't either. She couldn't wait another two minutes.

"I can go for help," Lucy offered.

Amanda wasn't about to argue. "Okay." She rubbed her stockinged feet with her hands, but that was only making them numb.

"I'll head for the crossroads and then onto the party. As soon as I see someone, I'll send them to get you."

Amanda nodded. "Good luck."

The two girls hugged, then Lucy cracked open her door. The wind howled into the car, bringing with it a dusting of snow. And then the door was closed and Lucy was gone.

Amanda rolled down her window. "Hurry back!" she said.

Lucy didn't turn around, only waved as she walked.

Amanda watched her friend disappear over a rise in the road, then she rolled up her window. Lucy was going to be a while, she thought.

She pulled her coat tight around her body, closed her eyes, and gave in to the urge to sleep.

When Amanda awoke, she couldn't feel her feet any more. She slipped her left foot out of its shoe to check if it was still there. It was. A little blue, a little stiff, but it was there.

She tried to move it and felt pain shoot up her leg.

She slipped her shoe back on – her beautiful shoe – and glanced at her watch.

11:30.

Oh, my God. Lucy had been gone for an hour and a half. Surely she would have made it to the party by now. What could have happened to her?

Amanda rolled down her window and looked out into the darkness. The snow was still falling, and there was six inches or more of it on the ground.

Where had Lucy gone?

She couldn't have forgotten about her. Maybe she'd been hit by a car, or lost her way, or . . .

Amanda began to cry, as much for Lucy as for herself. God, how could things have gone so wrong? She was so close to home. It was a couple of hours' walk in June, but now, in December . . .

She wiped a coat sleeve across her face to dry her eyes and decided that she had to walk to the crossroads. It couldn't be any worse than sitting here waiting. The party would be breaking up soon, and there would be all sorts of people driving by. She only had to make it to the crossroads, no more than five or six miles. She could make it.

After a deep breath, Amanda shut off the car's hazard lights, tightened the belt of her coat, and got out of the car.

The snow was deeper than she'd expected; it covered her ankles, even with the heels. But her feet and legs had already become numb to the cold, and she hardly felt the bite of snow against her skin.

"I can make it," she said aloud. "It won't be so bad."

And she began walking into the wind.

"Lucy!" She'd been calling out her name for the past . . . well, it seemed like a half-hour or more. "Lucy!"

She didn't really expect to get a reply, but it was something for her to do other than putting one foot in front of the other. Walking was usually something that was easy to do, something you took for granted. But Amanda couldn't feel her feet any more and had to trust that they were still beneath her, moving her along.

One foot in front of the other . . . in front of the other . . . in front of the other.

The cold had bitten into Amanda's face too. Her nose was cold steel and her cheeks blocks of ice.

"Lucy!"

"Mandy . . ."

The response had been weak, sliced to ribbons by the wind, but Amanda *had* heard it; she was sure of it.

"Lucy!"

"Over here."

Amanda followed the sound of Lucy's voice and found her lying in a ditch by the side of the road, half covered in newly fallen snow.

"What happened?"

"Thought I saw a car and started running," she said. "I ran off the road and fell down in here. I think my leg's broken. I can't move it."

Amanda saw that Lucy's left foot was bent at a funny angle, and her body began to tremble. She had been shivering for a long time, but this was an entirely different movement, one born out of fear.

"Hang on, I'll get you out."

Lucy began to laugh. "And do what?"

Amanda didn't know. It wasn't like she had a car to put her in, and she couldn't carry her. "Okay, I'll go for help. Stay where you are."

Lucy laughed again, or maybe she was crying.

Amanda turned back into the wind and resumed walking.

The crossroads was nowhere in sight.

It seemed to Amanda that she'd been walking for hours.

The road had become uneven, making it harder for her to stay on her feet. And three times the wind had knocked her down, each time making it that much harder for her to find her feet and put them back onto the road.

Her arms wouldn't move either. They were cold and frozen stiff in a tight hug around her body. Every movement brought new stabs of ice and wind to her cold, cold flesh.

Amanda's heart seemed to have slowed too, and the world around her had become blurry, the surrounding trees and falling snowflakes turning, turning, turning in a constant spiral around her.

Still she moved forward, thinking about the party and how everyone was going to love her legs and her new shoes.

Her shoes.

They were probably ruined by now.

She glanced down to look at her feet and realized that her right shoe was gone.

How long had she been walking like this?

The foot, bare now even of her hose, had turned black in the cold . . . like a dead thing.

No matter. She'd get a new pair of shoes. And then she'd

go to William Markham's party, and everyone would tell her she had nice legs and how pretty her new shoes were and how grown-up she looked.

As long as she kept walking, one foot in front of the other . . . in front of the . . .

A light appeared in the distance.

A tiny white light.

She began to run – awkwardly at first, but then her left shoe fell away, and she was able to stumble through the snow.

A light, a light . . .

Two now, in the distance.

She tried to wave, but her arm wouldn't move away from her body.

"Help," she shouted, but the words were carried away by the wind before they even left her mouth.

The lights were closer now.

"Please, help me," she cried, then she tripped on a stone hidden under the snow.

She tumbled and rolled across the road.

When she opened her eyes, the lights were gone.

So she stayed there in the middle of the road and sobbed.

The lights eventually returned, only now they were red and orange and flashing.

&

She awoke feeling . . . warm.

Toasty.

She took a deep breath and let out a long sigh.

Her father was there at her bedside. When he saw her open her eyes, he smiled. Her mother was farther away, sitting in a chair, crying into her hands.

"Hi, Dad."

"Hey, Mandy!"

"Am I in the hospital?"

Her dad nodded.

"And Lucy?"

"She's in the room next door."

"Is she okay? She hurt her leg."

Dad sighed. "She lost three of her toes, but she's going to be fine."

Amanda had to think about what she'd just heard. It sounded as if . . . "Three toes?"

"To frostbite," her father answered, trying to smile. "If you hadn't been so brave . . ." His voice trailed off, and he seemed to be fighting back tears.

Three toes to frostbite, she thought. *Wow*!

She tried to move her own toes, and it felt like they were there, wriggling beneath the sheets.

Felt *like* they were there.

A stab of fear pierced Amanda's heart. She struggled to lift her head off the pillow.

"Mandy, relax!" her father said, trying to calm her down.

"No, I want to see."

And her father's body went limp, as if there was no use in fighting it.

She looked down the bed, along the length of her body, and realized she looked short. The outline of her legs ended far from the end of the bed.

Her feet, she realized, were gone.

"It could have been worse," her father said.

Amanda wondered, How?

About the Contributors

Michael Arruda pens a movie column for the Horror Writers Association newsletter called "In the Spooklight." As a fiction writer, he has had his stories published in the anthologies *The Dead Inn*, *The Darkest Thirst*, and *New Traditions in Terror*. He makes his home in snowy New Hampshire, with his wife, Michelle, and their two sons.

Randy D. Ashburn is a judge who assesses workers' compensation claims in the Appalachian region of southeastern Ohio. Although he's been writing for just a short time, he's sold stories to such publications as *Night Terrors*, *Aboriginal Science Fiction*, and *Deep Outside*. He's also placed in the top twenty in the 1999 Writer's Digest Genre Short Story Contest and the Writers of the Future Contest.

Loren L. Barrett works as a library technician in children's and teen services in a southern Ontario public library. She has two cats of her own but takes care of a half-dozen others in the neighborhood. She likes to draw and heads a support group for families of children with diabetes. Her only previous publication was a poem in the Australian horror magazine *Blood Songs*.

Mark A. Garland hails from Syracuse, New York, where he lives with his wife and three children. Before becoming an author, he spent time as a rock musician and a race-car driver. He has published dozens of novels and short stories, including some set in the worlds of Star Trek and Dinotopia. He has also published a number of stories in anthologies edited by Bruce Coville.

Ed Greenwood is a large, jolly, bearded native of Ontario who's been hailed as the "Canadian author of the great American novel" and "an industry legend." An award-winning writer, game designer, and columnist, he's the creator of the Forgotten Realms fantasy world. Greenwood has published more than a hundred books and six hundred articles and short stories. His novels have sold millions of copies worldwide in more than a dozen languages. Recent titles include *Hand of Fire* and *A Dragon's Ascension*.

Born in Halifax, Nova Scotia, **Tanya Huff** now lives on a farm in rural Ontario. She is one of Canada's best-selling authors of fantasy fiction, and she has more than a dozen titles in print. Some of her most popular novels are those in the Blood series of fantastic mysteries. These feature the former policewoman Victoria Nelson and her sometime partner, a 450-year-old vampire named Henry Fitzroy.

Michael Kelly's fiction has appeared in a wide range of magazines and anthologies, including *Be Afraid!*, the *Carleton Arts Review*, *Deadbolt*, *The Literary Journal*, *Northern Horror*, and *Space* *and Time*. He lives with his wife, the poet Carolyn MacDonell, and their two children in Pickering, Ontario.

David Nickle has had stories published in many anthologies, including *Wild Things Live Here*, *Northern Horror*, and *Northern Suns*. He's a past winner of the Bram Stoker Award (with Edo van Belkom, for their story "Rat Food"). His novel *The Claus Effect* (based on an Aurora Award–winning short story), co-written with Karl Schroeder, is available from Tesseract Books. He lives and works in Toronto.

Tom Piccirilli is the author of ten horror and mystery novels, including *A Lower Deep*, *Hexes*, *The Deceased*, *The Dead Past*, *Sorrow's Crown*, and *The Night Class*. He's also sold more than one hundred stories in the horror, mystery, and fantasy fields, and he is a recipient of the Bram Stoker Award and a final nominee for the World Fantasy Award.

Since 1988, **Edmund Plante** has published twenty-five young adult horror novels with the German publisher Cora Verlag. In North America, he's published several horror novels for young readers, including *Alone in the House* and *Last Date*, and adult novels such as *Garden of Evil* and *Trapped*. A resident of Webster, Massachusetts, he has also had many short stories published in such magazines and anthologies as the *Portland Review*, *Haunts*, *Dark Regions*, and *Be Afraid!*

Michael Rowe is the three-time Lambda Literary Award–nominated author and editor of eight books, including the essay collection *Looking for Brothers* and the horror anthology *Queer Fear*. An award-winning journalist and National Magazine Award finalist, Rowe has had his work appear in publications like the *National Post*, the *Globe and Mail*, and *The*

Advocate. He lives in Toronto with his life partner, Brian McDermid. His Web site is www.michaelrowe.com.

Robert J. Sawyer, of Mississauga, Ontario, is the only writer to win the top science-fiction awards of the United States (the Nebula), France (the Grand Prix de l'Imaginaire), Spain (Premio UPC de Ciencia Ficción), and Japan (Seiun). In addition, he has won the Aurora for both his short fiction and his novels, as well as the Arthur Ellis Award from the Crime Writers of Canada for best short story. His novels include *The Terminal Experiment*, *Factoring Humanity*, and *Homonids*. You can visit his Web site at www.sfwriter.com.

Edo van Belkom has won the Bram Stoker and Aurora awards for his fiction. His two hundred short stories have been published in everything from *Truck News* to *Year's Best Horror*. His twenty books include the novels *Lord Soth*, *Teeth*, and *Martyrs*; the collections *Death Drives a Semi* and *Six-Inch Spikes*; and the non-fiction books *Writing Horror* and *Northern Dreamers*. He lives in Brampton, Ontario. His Web page is located at www.vanbelkom.com.

Sheri White is a resident of Maryland, where she makes her home with her husband, children, and two cats. She is the author of more than twenty short stories, which have been published in a wide variety of small-press magazines. "Wasting Away" is her first professional sale. Her Web site can be reached at www.geocities.com/sheriw1965/index.html.